One Too Many Drinks

A disturbing journey into a world of unrepressed Sex
and unattainable Love

George Howell

First paperback edition July 2019

Book design by George Howell

ISBN 978-1-7331992-0-9 (paperback)

Table of Contents

Chapter 1:
One Foot off the Tight Rope

"LET'S ALL MEET AT THE BAR"

It was a Friday before a 3-day weekend Geremy, Carl and Dave are at a bar.

Geremy speaks, "Gentleman, Let's raise our glasses to Friday. Freedom for 3-days. So, what's on the agenda."

Carl replies, "I can't stay late tonight, Stacy and I are getting away for the whole 3 days".

Geremy replies, "and where did you find this one?"

"You guys know Stacy?"

The other two men replied in surprise, "Stacy? Stacy in Accounting!", "When did this start?'

"It's been a week or so."

"Or so!! ... "said Geremy"...You DOG! You've been keeping secrets from us? "

Dave replies, "SWEET! I like Stacy"

Geremy tries to regain the topic and says to Dave, "How about you? You free for the night. "

"I'll roll for a while, have to get up early in the morning—taking the family camping. The kids have been bugging me for a while, but for tonight I will be your Wingman. "Cool, alright, let's see what's in this place."

As they tap glasses and set gaze around the bar and towards the dance floor, a stranger sits down next to them, orders a beer and initiates a conversation. "What's up guys I could not help overhearing your conversation. I came to town for a meeting, and I'm stuck over the weekend. You sound like you know the places to go, mind if I enjoy the hunt with you.

The stranger was well dressed, a good physique, and could hold a conversation. The perfect combination to penetrate a lair of women.

Carl gives the nod of approval and says, "Well that sounds like my queue to exit. I'm going to tie up with Stacy and get our weekend escape on." Dave perked up and asked the bartender for another round and to include our newly found hunter. They drank, shared stories, laughed, and searched around for possibilities to approach. Dave spoke to the group again "I'm out after I finish this one, don't do anything I wouldn't do!" They all laughed, "Yeah, Mr. Married with Kids, that leaves everything wide open."

"Yeah, Yeah, Yeah, one day, you will be there too. Stranger, I pass over the role of Wingman to you."

Carl and Dave leave the bar, but not before hearing, "I want a full report next week on the weekend escape."

"Well my new friend, my name is Geremy with a G, it looks like it's just you and me, what's your name. "

"Austin"

Geremy thought to himself what a great name to finish off the visual, it could be a lucky night.

"Austin, that's a good name to attract women. Where you from?"

"Michigan."

"Wow, Welcome to Sacramento."

As the night moved on, Austin proved to be a great icebreaker with the ladies and a great wingman. This continued as they stumbled from Bar to Bar on the strip. When evening began to twinkle into the next day, Austin suggested that they sit and have another drink before he goes back to the hotel bar to see if the lady who was also from another state was still there. Austin said, "but before I go, let me tell you about this sexual encounter I did that will blow your mind. Last year I was on this extreme kayaking trip with my wife, her kayak flipped, and while she was rolling it, she hit her head on some rocks. I pulled her out and started giving her mouth to mouth. I could feel her life slipping from her. After a while, my lungs were aching, and she was non-responsive and not breathing. My mouth to mouth efforts turned into deep kissing, and the next thing I knew I was zipping down her wetsuit and making love to her lifeless body, and I kept going even though she was dead. It was the best sexual experience of my life. No living woman has ever brought me close to that experience. I don't know why I'm telling you this, but I'll leave you with that thought. Later dude"

Geremy pondered on that reveal over the next drink. Wondering am I so drunk that I heard it wrong or did this guy just tell me that he fucked his dead wife. That was so beyond Geremy's imagination.

Well, the weekend played out very much the same for Geremy, jumping from bar to bar, one-night stands, breakfast in the morning — repeat.

Chapter 2:
When Darkness Pulls

The next business day Geremy could only think about informing his friends about the necrophilia tag along on Friday. He told the story again and again. He said it so much it turned into a joke:

Three guys go into a bar and talk about their weekend sexual experience, the first guy says "I had a great night I fucked my ex-girlfriend", the second says "I had a horrible night I fucked my ex-wife," and the third says "I had the most satisfying night ever I fucked my dead wife", the other two looked at him and said "how was that satisfying", the third guy replied "I only had to please myself"

Weeks have gone by since his evening with Austin, and the one thing that continues to linger is what he said about no lady since that experience has ever pleased him. This notion of never being satisfied, to a man like Geremy - whose entire sexual career is centered around one-night romances, was incredibly foreign. How could fucking someone, you say that you

Love, while the life left their body be a pleasant experience or was the thought of it being the last time acting as an Aphrodisiac. The more he thought on it, the higher his desire to experience it became.

It was changing him. He was starting to explore the darker side of sex, like erotic asphyxiation. He thought that if the experience was as close to death as possible, then he too could have that ultimate experience of sexual pleasure. He stepped away from his usual Friday nights with Carl and Dave and stepped into the fetish world of the people living in the shadows.

In the days to follow while walking in the halls of the office, Dave stopped Carl, "you know Geremy better than I do, I'm becoming a bit worried for him, does he seem different to you."

"It's more than different, I stopped in his office to borrow a pen and saw one of those Sadist face masks in it. The man is into some sick shit, and I don't want any part of it."

"but he's our friend… shouldn't we at least have a talk with him before cutting him off."

"HE CUT US OFF..."

"lower your voice."

'he cut us off, no more Friday's, no communication of any kind outside of work. How do you think you're going to get to talk to him"?

"True, we probably will not be able to catch up with him after work. So, let's try to get him out to lunch."

"Go ahead, if you can set it up, I'll be there."

It took close to a month to finally get Geremy to agree to lunch, with each passing day you could see the darkness growing in him. His weekend escapades have evolved to nightly occurrences. He looks like he barely sleeps.

"What's cooking guys, it's been a while. I've been so busy," said Geremy.

" No joke, I was telling Dave that you must have gotten secretly married and you were too afraid to let us know."

"But seriously, where have you been. We know it's not your workload. Remember, as the only married man, I live my life vicariously through your tales of conquest. My life has gotten boring— give me some tales."

"Nothing to tell, I've moved on to different clubs that you may not feel comfortable in."

"Do they have alcohol? Do they have women? Or is this your subtle way to say you've switched to men."

"Ease up Carl, I'm married, and you've been seeing Stacy pretty steadily now. Maybe these new clubs offer too many temptations and Geremy's trying to protect our relationships, Right?"

"Let's just say that I'm in search of that earth-shattering sexual pleasure that will put me in the same boat you guys are in, captured by the heart."

"You mean he was captured by the dick or bondage or whipped or whatever other crazy shit you've been doing. Look were supposed to be Boyz and the other day I was walking in the hall and needed a pen to sign a paper, so I dipped into your office to borrow a pen and saw your mask. You're into that fetish shit now!"

"I'm trying the darker side of my sexual cravings; you know, turning it up a notch."

"I'm glad you left us out."

"Shut-up Dave!" "That fetish shit corrupts your soul. You never find happiness only more demented ways to hurt yourself or others. You know what, you haven't been right since you met that dude at the bar - Austin. He put that thought in your mind of finding the ultimate sexual pleasure as he found in fucking his dead wife. Is that what you're looking for. Well, news flash, you have to get married, find true love, and then have her die in a freak accident. And how close are you to that?"

"Maybe your right, and I've been trying to get there the wrong way."

"Stop, you mean Carl's right. You're still hung up on that Austin Tale. Hell, you don't even know if that was True. He was just a stranger at the bar."

"You weren't there, you didn't see his face as he told me what happened. It was true, but if the only way that I can reach that is to find true love. Then I need you to help put me back on the rope, cause I've fallen down into some wild shit."

"I got you, we got you."

Over the months to follow Geremy filled them in on the types of things he was doing, Carl and Dave were shocked and in awe of the things he told them. To rid him of the dark desires they knew, he had to embrace the right love aspect just as profoundly as the dark side. Geremy had to set his mind on the long game and to get there, we needed to know what type of woman his true love is. So, they told him how they found their true love.

"Hey, Dave, what brought you and your wife together."

"Jasmine and I were high school sweethearts, but we actually have known each other all of our lives. She was the girl next door. I'm 1 year older so you could say that she was born for me. Although it did not start that way. Before high school, she was this annoying girl next door, that wanted to go everywhere I went. She was tough, she played baseball and football with us and could beat up most of the boys in the community. She was an only child. I had noticed a change in her in junior high and a change in how I felt

11

too, but during my last year, 8th grade, she became a woman in my eyes. I've seen her dress up for Sunday church with some makeup on but this day she had everything working, tight jeans with heels, hair down and fluffy with a little curl and a face that begged you to want to kiss her. So, I did, and I never left her side after that. My lips have never touched another woman's lips nor ever wanted too."

"Wow, that's talking from your heart, Geremy did you see Dave's face while he was talking, he wasn't doing an accounting of the last night adventure, he was reliving the past right before our eyes. I never asked you, Dave, where did you grow up?"

"Ohio"

"O-HI-O. So you grew up on a farm— milking cows, fresh eggs from the chicken's, that kind of living."

"Not everybody, Carl, from Ohio lived on a farm we lived in the suburbs—a nice house with a decent yard."

"and only one girl in your life, was it some kind of religious cult thing—thou must stay with the first girl you kiss or burn in hell for eternity"?

"you can be a complete ass sometimes. So Geremy did you have any childhood flings or crushes."

"There was this one girl, but we stayed as friends."

"Oh no, not a 'let us be friends' story."

"shut up, Carl, tell the story, Geremy."

"Like you, she was the girl next door, I was 2 years older, and her family owned the largest house with the most property. Despite all of that we became the very best friends. I watched her go from this skinny flat chested wimpy girl to Captain of the cheerleaders, a gymnastic star and then to an advertising genius. "

"So, you tried, and she shot you down."

"No, I never tried. Back then, I was this shy kid. I was too afraid to try, I did not want to be shot down and have to see her at school and home every day after that. But I did I guess, secretly love her. We talked about everything, all her boyfriend problems, her first kiss, her tough parents. She set me up on my first date. Maybe that's when it all began, I remember the look on her face when I walked away with the other girl. She did not have as big of a smile that she had when setting

13

everything up, it was like she was saying goodbye. So, the next day I told her it was nice but not the right girl for me. She smiled really bright and said OK, let's find somebody else. All the girls from that point on have been a one-time date."

" What was her name?"

"Angelica. I called her Angel, everyone else used Angie."

"Have you kept in touch."

 "I think she works for one of the advertising firms downtown."

Geremy knew that she was a VP of the largest advertising firm downtown and lived on the top floor Penthouse of the most sort after luxury condos. She had done quite well for herself. She reached out to him a few years back after attending the funeral of his dad, he never replied back.

"Well, it sounds to me like this one could be your true love. Are you still interested? Is she single?"

"Guys, that ship has already sailed. Regardless of how I may feel today, too many years have passed. Seriously, don't go there, in fact, I think I can find my way from here. Bringing back these old feelings is setting the tone for what I am looking for in true love. Thanx for pulling me back out of the darkness."

Chapter 3:
Secrets

Things settled down to a new normal, and the 3 amigos were happy. Geremy threw away his one-night stand outlook, and after quite a few encounters, he's found someone that can hold his interest. It's been 5 months, and he seems to be happy.

"Hey guys, I need a big favor. Tell me you have no plans for this weekend."

"Carl, you sound crazy. What's up?"

"Well, I'm going to pop the question to Stacy this weekend and thought we could all get together and celebrate after."

Geremy quickly responded, "I won't say congrats until she officially says, Yes."

"Tell me when & where, and Jasmine and I will be there."

Carl set up a flash mob engagement event at the Sacramento Downtown Grid Area.

It was a blast, the entire performance took about 45 minutes, and Stacy was in tears as she said, yes. They are planning a To Be Determined destination wedding. Throughout the whole engagement celebration, you could see Geremy occasionally gaze away in a similar manner that he said Angelica had when he left on his first set-up date. What could be troubling him so? It's hard to tell with Geremy.

Geremy had to place his mother in a home when her dementia became more than she could control, not a choice that pleased him, but due to the travel distance, the train and his working schedule it was the best option. Inevitably, he moved back into his father's house and brought his mother home on weekends. This did not fare well with maintaining a love life, but he was comfortable for now. For Geremy, caring for his mother in her time of need brought a greater sense of accomplishment, dedication, and responsibility. It also removed him from the city releasing an enormous amount of pressure and temptation.

One year later, his mother passed. Everyone from the community and loved ones from far away attended the funeral. Amidst the attendees there was a personal surprise to Geremy, it was Angelica. Seeing her took him back to his growing up years and now standing before him was the True Love of his life.

Angelica had a few secrets of her own. Unknown to everyone in the community, including her parents and Geremy, Angelica was secretly married. He was not the type of person her father would have approved of, but they were madly in love with each other. He was her knight in shining armor in a fireman's uniform. Angelica was in a car accident where she was pinned in a taxi under a petroleum truck that was leaking its fuel. Harry was the first responder that found her and carried her from the scene. She suffered no significant injuries, but they kept in touch and secretly married. She asked Harry not to attend the funeral, she felt that at the burial of a good friend / 2nd mother would not be the ideal time to spring this on everyone, that whole mixed emotion thing or was it because she had not told Geremy yet.

She helped Geremy to close down the house and encouraged him to go back to his condo in the city for a little while to clear his head. Geremy talked about meeting up for dinner from time to time, and Angelica said that her job usually keeps her very busy, but we'll see. So, with the closing of the house complete, they stayed that evening and boarded the first train in the morning to head back to the city.

It was Tuesday morning, before dawn and the train was empty, yet it stopped at all the stops and no-one boarded. On the way into the city, there was a one-mile-long section that traveled through a tunnel. Angelica was claustrophobic and always hated that section. Geremy remembered this and asked, "Are you still nervous about going through the tunnel?".

"Shush! Yes, and thank you for bringing it up."

"Sorry"

As the train approached the entrance of the tunnel, there was a rumble on the track. Geremy said, "Did you feel that"

"Geremy, I can't believe you. Seriously, you're going to try and frighten me more than I already am."

Angelica was already embracing her fears with her eyes closed, and her body so tight that she did not feel the extra motion. While in the tunnel, the motion increased to a violent tossing, it was an earthquake. Angelica started screaming, placing her hands to her face while Geremy, too afraid to let go of the bars, kept begging for her to hold on tightly to the bars of the seat. A huge section of the tunnel came crashing down, crushing the train car in front of their section, and everything went dark. Angelica was thrown from her seat through the air. The remainder of the tunnel came down around them, sealing them in like a mausoleum. Trapped, no way out, no cellphone service, completely alone. You could hear the stress on the metal of their train section with heavy concrete resting on the top and the sides. Geremy reached over to Angelica, unaware that she had been tossed, feeling about noticing that she was no longer next to him he yelled out to her, "Angel, are you OK, Angel answer me, I'm coming". Geremy turns on the flashlight on his phone to look around. To his horror, Angelica had been thrown through the air and into the front wall of the train car. He could see that she was bleeding from her head and arms. As Geremy knelt down to Angelica, it appeared that she was not breathing. He placed his fingers to her neck, and she barely had a pulse. Here before him was the girl that made his heart skip a beat now a woman lying the floor battered and dying before him. He immediately positioned her body properly for CPR and began 30 chest compressions and 2 rescue breaths ...repeat ...repeat. He continued, his arms were tiring, and he was starting to get dizzy from the excessive short rescue breaths. He checked her pulse; it was getting weaker, and she was not responding to the CPR. He continued, and as his lips came in contact with hers, he started having flashbacks of their childhood and how much he really wanted to kiss her then. Back to chest compressions ...25,26,27,28,29,30 back to rescue breaths 1,2 repeat. After a while, the 2 rescue breaths became kisses, and his compressions turned into fondling of her breast. Geremy's thoughts now moved to Austin, this is the same situation he was in when his wife was dying from the kayaking accident. This is my chance to experience the same ultimate pleasure with my true love.

Breast Fondling ...28,29,30 ... Kisses... repeat. At that moment, another tremor was felt, and the train metal gave out a loud noise from all the wait on it. Geremy thought perhaps this train is his death song, Austin's story rang even louder in his head.

Breast Fondling ...10,11,12 ... Kissing, kissing, kissing, and then Geremy did the unthinkable. Here before him the person of all his childhood and adult dreams, the woman who he had the ultimate respect for, now lies on the train floor showing her naked body filled with his discretion. He did not feel the sensation that Austin spoke of. Instead, he felt anger upon himself, disgust for the act performed, betrayal to Angelica, and no longer the feelings of man but that of a horned beast. Geremy wanted the train car to collapse at that moment, taking their lives, but it did not. He re-dressed Angelica, and although she still was not breathing, she still had a weak pulse. He sat and stared at her still body and could not touch her, no more CPR.

Chapter 4:
The Miracle

Geremy did not know about the secret wedding nor that her husband was a first responder or that Angelica had placed a call to him before they left on the train. As he sat staring at her, the sounds that he thought were the train on the verge of collapsing was the sound of first responders working on getting them out. The last of the concrete sections were removed, and the jaws of life pried open the doors, there stood Harry.

"You must be Geremy. Please step back. "

As they placed her body on to the lifting board and carried her out. Geremy asked, "how did you know my name."

"I'm her husband."

Geremy was very meticulous in the manner that he redressed her. Cleaning her vaginal area from the disgust that he had placed there. He pulled her panties up, keeping them smooth and not bunched, he carefully arranged her breasts back into her bra and closed the latch. Angelica was wearing a button-downed dress, and he pulled it down around her to fit as though she was standing up as he buttoned it closed. She looked like his Angel again even though he knew he could never call her that again. The paramedics took them in separate ambulances to the hospital, Harry rode with Angelica.

Angelica and Harry had decided to freeze some of her eggs because she was going to turn 32 on her next birthday. Their appointment was set for Friday at the Northern California Fertility Medical Center. The freezing process takes three weeks in which the first two weeks included an Anti-Mullerian Hormone and Antral Follicle Count to measure the ovarian egg reserve. Also, during these two weeks, Angelica had to inject herself with fertility meds to allow for multiple eggs to mature in her ovaries. Harry was capable and willing to enter any fire, crash through any wall, and even swim the deepest sea to be Angelica's first responder, but he could not administer her injections. The last step of all their efforts was a scheduled 15-minute office visit on Friday for eggs extraction.

Harry's thoughts were on both his wife and her wish to freeze her, so, eggs called their fertility doctor from the ambulance and explained everything. She asked to speak with the paramedic and introduced herself as Angelica's doctor. They talked for a few moments, and the cellphone was returned to Harry.

Dr. Sharindha explained to Harry that his wife was not going to survive; in fact, she has already passed. The paramedics are not authorized to pronounce a victim as dead. She asked Harry to instruct the ambulance driver to reroute the ambulance to the medical center, there still could be time to extract the eggs.

"Please take us quickly to the Northern California Fertility Medical Center."

The paramedic yelled out to her partner, "Reroute our course, go to the Northern California Fertility Medical Center, I know the place, it's straight up route 80 about 5 mins."

Dr. Sharindha and her team were waiting at the door and took her in immediately.

"Harry. Please sit here and attend to the paperwork. We have her."

"Set up the ultrasound and let's see what we are dealing with. "

Unfortunately, the additional injuries that Angelica's body had to withstand damaged the eggs that were in her ovaries. In scanning the rest of the area, they noticed an egg in her uterus — a fertilized egg.

"Quickly get her body on life support and the mechanical heart while we find a surrogate carrier for the egg."

Dr. Sharindha rushed through the halls to get to Harry, "Harry, we're not able to save the eggs; however, I have wonderful news. There is a fertile egg in Angelica's uterus, we must move quickly. Had you and Angelica discussed any plans for a backup surrogate to carry your child through the developing and birthing process."

"No, we thought that we had a lot of time before we would need something like that, but wait, are you telling me that I have a child on the way."

"It's still very early, but if we can find a surrogate quickly and have no complications in transferring, it is a possibility. Would you like for us to look through our surrogate listing to find you a match?"

"Yes, please save my child." then a moment of silence comes over Harry. "Can I go to Angelica?"

"Oh my God, Yes, Harry, she's right in here."

Harry stayed with Angelica the rest of the day into the night only to be awoken by Dr. Sharindha the next morning with great news. They found the perfect surrogate.

"That's excellent news. When will the transfer take place "?

"This afternoon."

"and the support systems."

"they will stay intact while we perform the extraction."

"and then" Harry takes a deep breath, "she'll be gone."

"Oh, Harry, Angelica has already left us. These machines make things seem like there is hope. Angelica died on the train."

Here now is this chiseled first responder dropping back into his seat grabbing the hand of his wife, his friend, his True Love - relinquishing his strong stature in a puddle of tears and painful groans.

"Harry, I know this is hard, but I need to ask you, the surrogate for your child is here, and she would like to meet you before signing the papers. May I bring her in."

Harry took a deep breath, wiped his eyes, and pulled on his inner strength to compose himself for the introduction.

"Yes, you can bring her in."

"Harry, this is Margarite"

"Hello Harry, I wanted to say that I am so sorry for your lost. I do not drink or use drugs. I will be the best surrogate for your child and deliver a child to you that will be healthy and strong. "

Margarite was a stunning woman 5'8" with a body and face of a top model. Harry barely looked at her but was comforted by her words.

"I'm sure you will be a fantastic surrogate, and the life of my child is what I have to live for, that's my future. "

"Dr. Sharindha, please take care of my child. I must go make plans to put my wife to rest."

Chapter 5:
Hello Mom and Dad

Angelica had always been the event planner between them, and Harry had no idea how to set up a funeral, who to invite, how do I tell her parents. At that moment he remembered that Geremy just buried his mother and as one of Angelica's close friends perhaps he could help. He pulled some favors and got Geremy's telephone number from the hospital he was taken too.

Harry kissed Angelica and set out to find Geremy. He made contact on the telephone and made plans to meet that afternoon at Starbucks.

"Hi, Geremy, thank you for coming, I know you don't know me, but I need your assistance."

"Ok, but first, what did you mean about you being Angelica's husband."

"Angelica and I married a year and a half ago, secretly. She said that her parents would not approve of her seeing a fireman let alone marry one, so we secretly eloped. So now, I have to plan for her funeral, and I have no clue where to start."

"We start with telling her parents."

"yeah, will you go with me? We need to leave tonight, I'll drive."

The two men brought together by circumstance head off to inform Angelica's parents that they will never see their daughter again. On the ride, Harry talked about Angelica the whole way. He said he fell in love with her the moment he looked into the window of her trapped car. She came down to the firehouse a week later said she wanted to thank me. So, they went out to dinner and haven't been apart since. Geremy was getting more disgusted with each word that Harry spoke, he wanted him to shut up. To Geremy, you didn't know her as he did, you didn't grow up with her, you rescued her from a bad situation and took advantage of her gratitude. Harry kept talking about the life they were building. Harry said that never in his wildest dreams would he have thought that such a beautiful, successful woman could love him. She told me about you, she said when you were growing up that she really liked you. She said that you only wanted to be her friend and how the day that she set you up on your first date, nearly tore her heart apart.

"I guess I should be thanking you, had you wanted to be more than friends, you would probably be married to her and not me."

Geremy replied, "Imagine that, but we both miss her now."

"Yes, we do… but I have a way to enjoy her presence in the future."

"You mean thru your memories like you've been spilling out this whole drive."

"I guess I have been talking a lot. Knowing that amid this whole nightmare, there is a miracle. Angelica was taking fertility injections to increase her egg generation so that we could freeze a few for later use. The doctor said that I must have had one determined sperm cell hanging around that fertilized the only egg that fell as a result of the accident."

"What are you saying?"

"At this moment Dr. Sharindha is extracting the fertilized egg and implanting my child into a surrogate mother."

Harry's cellphone plays a melody, "Hello."

"Harry, it's Dr. Sharindha. The procedure is complete, and the surrogate and egg are resting. We will know in the next 48 hours if the egg has properly secured itself in her uterus."

"Thank you, Doctor,"

"let's see how things go. I hope you won't mind, but our center does not have the capability of housing a body, so I called a local funeral home to take Angelica's body. I will send you the contact information."

"Thank you again."

"I placed all of her personal items in a bag here at the office. In her pocket I found her wedding rings, it too will be in the bag. I am so sorry, Harry."

"Thank you."

Harry places the phone down and goes silent. Geremy stays silent also. In his mind, he was constructing his own story, if she was on fertility pills could I be the father. He had so many questions with no answers.

"Turn here" as Geremy breaks the silence "the house is about a quarter mile through the gate."

Harry parks the car at the front door. The two men turn to each other, take a deep breath, and exit the vehicle. As they approached the front door, Angelica's father opens it, "Geremy what brings you here and who's with you."

Geremy begins to reply, and Harry cuts in, "Mr. Olswain, I'm Harry Albert ..." at that moment, Mrs. Olswain opens the door wider and says, "fireman Harry?" To Harry's surprise. "Angelica told you about me."

"She told her mother, I found out yesterday. So where is she, hiding in the car?" Mr. Olswain shouts "come out of the car now, we all know."

Geremy with a low voice, says, "She's not in the car."

Harry speaks, "There was an accident ..." Mr. Olswain interrupts "Yes, we know how you met," Harry continues "... No, there's been another accident."

Mrs. Olswain starts crying, and Mr. Olswain runs to the car screaming, "Come out, I know you're in there, come out." He slams his fist on the car and turns to the two men and with a calmer shaky voice, "Let's go inside and sit down."

They walked into the house, on the left wall is a large family portrait of Angelica and her parents. The foyer emptied out into a large room with 2 sitting areas. We proceeded through the center of the room between the 2 sitting areas under a large archway leading into the kitchen, we sat looking out of a 2-story high-multiple pane-bay window. Mr. Olswain explained how this was Angelica's favorite place to sit and look upon the fields. Here she felt like a princess looking out on her realm. Mrs. Olswain offered us coffee or drinks, and then they sat. An awkward silence came on to all of us. Mr. Olswain was reflecting back condemning himself for the fact that Angelica would think that he would step in the way of her true happiness regardless of her man's status, was I that shallow in her eyes. Here I stand with a fault that I no longer have a chance to correct. As father's, we tend to place thoughts in our daughters' minds to help them to make good decisions in a mate while growing up. Sometimes, we forget to remove these thoughts when they get older. I guess that's because, for us, they never stop being our little girl. But because of my blindness, I was denied the very moment that all fathers dream of, giving his daughter away at the altar and our first/last dance.

Mrs. Olswain reflected the pain of the entire situation in her body language. The woman that came to the door bellowing with excitement to meet "fireman Harry" with a smile that was brighter than the stars and the full moon that graced the sky, now looked as though she had aged 10 years in a moment. Her heart was simply ripped from her chest as she sits slumped over, crying like a child that had just fallen for the first time wanting to be picked up.

With tears still in their eyes, Mr. Olswain spoke with a trembling voice that he had to clear several times— "So Harry, please tell us what-when-how this happened, was she in any pain, did she leave any parting words for us. "

Harry just as tearful as they were responded "I wish I could answer your questions; I have the same thoughts myself, but Geremy was with her. They were traveling home from his mother's funeral when the earthquake struck.

Geremy spoke in a low voice, with no tears in his eyes, "Well, after we finished cleaning up the house and covering the furniture, we left for the train the next morning. We boarded the last section, and as we rode, we rehashed some of the fun times from the past. I remembered that she was claustrophobic, and I asked if the train tunnel still scared her. She angerly yelled at me, letting me know that it does, and thanked me for reminding her that it was coming. She then asked if I can remember so much about her, why was it that I never asked her out on a date. She said she was waiting.

That's when I felt the first rumbling, I asked her if she could feel it, Angelica thought that I was trying to scare her. We did a lot of that when we were younger. The rumblings continued, only this time she felt them, I told her to hold on to the seat posts. She became hysterical, the rumbling became violent. There was a tremendous crashing noise, everything went dark. I clinched my seat post as tight as I could, and a surge of motion came from behind, trying to throw me forward. I reached over for Angelica, and she was gone. I turned on my cell phone light, and she wasn't in the seat. The train section was in shambles, some of the benches were pulled from the floorboards, poles twisted and broken, and as I started making my way to the front of the section, I could see her. She was lying on the floor amidst the rubble that was thrown to the front. She must have been thrown about 30 feet. I yelled to her with no response. When I reached her, she was unconscious with a very faint pulse, I tried administering CPR with no response. "

Mrs. Olswain cried out, "STOP! my poor baby." Tears streamed down her face, she made an attempt to stand and fell back into her seat. Mr. Olswain nestled her in his arms and said to Geremy, "I'm glad you were there, at least she was not alone". He thanked both of them for coming here to tell them.

Mrs. Olswain, "Have you made any plans for her body"?

Harry responded, "I have not made plans for her burial. Angelica was the planner; I don't know what to do."

Mrs. Olswain asked, "Harry, would you mind if I brought her back home. I will take care of all the arrangements."

"No, I do not mind and Thank you. I do need to share something else with you, a ray of hope to brighten these darkest of times. Angelica would have been 32 on her next birthday and since children were not in our plan yet she, no we, decided to freeze some of her eggs to be used when we're ready. This Friday, we were supposed to have had them extracted and placed into storage. The accident destroyed most of her eggs, but by the Grace of GOD, one was found attached to the walls of her uterus fertilized. The doctor at the fertility center was able to transfer the fertile egg to a surrogate mother. We will know if the transfer was successful in the next 48 hrs. You may be grandparents soon."

Mrs. Olswain rose up from her husband's lap, and her face had a glow as though touched by an angel, "Oh my God, my baby's baby. Who is the Surrogate, Can I meet her"?

"No worries Mrs. Olswain, I will set it up once we know for sure."

She turned to her husband and gave him a kiss while embracing him, she grabbed Harry's hand and said, "We have a second chance to raise another exceptional child, our miracle baby. Please, it's late, stay over tonight."

The two men accepted the invitation to stay over. Harry went on to explain what transpired in the ambulance that led to their redirecting it to the Fertility Center.

Geremy continued to wonder, was it Harry's miracle baby or was it his. Could this baby, pulled from the grasp of death, be his seed. Geremy wanted to jump up in jubilation and pronounce that this, soon to be a miracle, was his. A child born from the unexploited love that they shared for each other growing up. The more he thought on it, the more he convinced himself that the despicable deed that he had performed was heaven-directed, his Kismet and this soon to be child would be his escape out of the darkness that had consumed him. His purpose now is on how to claim this child as his own. I need to derive a plan and a time to start on it. I know, I'll wait until after the child is born.

The next morning was Friday, the day that the eggs were deemed to be extracted and now that same afternoon they will find out if the transfer was successful. Mrs. Olswain woke up and made a large breakfast of pancakes, bacon, eggs, toast, potato pancakes, fresh cut berries, coffee, tea, freshly squeezed orange and mango juice. Yes, she had been up for hours. The men in the house walked down to a magnificent display of edible desires.

"Please, sit and eat. I was thinking Harry, perhaps you could stay for the day and we could hear the news together. Please tell me you can do that."

Harry quickly responded, "That would be nice. "then he paused and looked at Geremy "Let me not be rude, Geremy do you need to get back."

Geremy already tired of hearing their excited voices responded slowly, "Well I do have a few things this afternoon."

Mr. Olswain, with no hesitation, said "Then it is settled we are going to spend a day in the city. After we complete this wonderful breakfast. Let's take to our cars and drive to the city, this way we can see our daughter, see where our daughter was sharing her life with you, then go to the Fertility Center and get the news."

Mrs. Olswain said, "Well, let me go and get ready while you eat."

Mr. Olswain called out to Macie as she started up the stairs, "Macie make sure you get Charlie's telephone number at the funeral home, so he can pick up Angelica."

Chapter 6:
She wanted You

The men enjoyed their breakfast, and the conversation moved away from Angelica.

As they approached the cars, Mrs. Olswain asked to ride with Harry and Geremy rode with Mr. Olswain. Harry reminded Mrs. Olswain to put on her seatbelt. She thanked him and asked him to call her Macie.

"I guess you're asking yourself why I wanted to ride with you.

I wanted to let you know that Angelica talked to me about you every day from the time you rescued her. She told me about the accident and this amazing man who helped her out of the car. The look in your eyes and your smile made her feel safe. A face that she could not get out of her mind, I convinced her to find you and thank you for your deed. You gave her the strength to come out of her protective shell. A feeling she had not felt for a long time, since her dream days of Geremy. Yes, before meeting you, she still wanted Geremy, the boy who captured her heart in grade school. So, seeing the two of you together at my door last night was quite a shock and of course, what followed was just devastating. How long have you known Geremy?"

"I met him 1 hour before coming to see you. Angelica never spoke of him until the news came of his mother's passing and all she said then was that he was a childhood friend. Angelica wanted to attend the funeral alone so that she could break the news of us to her Dad. I guess she wanted to break it to Geremy as well."

"Geremy was always a little shy, in fact, Angelica set up his first date. She came home afterward and ran to her room in tears. I came in to comfort her, she was distraught asking How could he go out with her. I said Honey isn't that what you wanted – she said no, he was supposed to want me.

I'm telling you this Harry because in the house I was noticing how Geremy was looking at you, he looked angry. Be careful around him. Before Angelica met you she thought that she had seen Geremy across the street from her home a couple of times - stalking. Know this, my daughter loved you, and she would tell me how you made her feel loved."

Meanwhile, in the other car, Mr. Olswain asked, "So how long have you known Harry?

Geremy responded, "I don't."

"what do you mean, the two of you came to my house together, he seemed very comfortable speaking with you. So, Angelica never told you about him."

Mr. Olswain had a way of getting straight to the point with few words. Geremy always felt uncomfortable around him. If he could have avoided riding with him, he would have.

"No, Angelica never mentioned him. My first time meeting him was when the doors of that train were pried open. He was the first to enter, and he told me to stand back away from her, while they took her body out. He had me placed in a different ambulance, and I did not see him again until 1 hour before we came to you. Hell, I don't even know how he got my information."

"Geremy, you sound like your angry or are your jealous of this guy, you think he stole your girl. Your pathetic, you had your chance to make my daughter happy, and you blew it. This guy may not be who I envisioned for my daughter, but after meeting and talking to him and feeling the love that he has for her, I like him. He's a real man."

Geremy muttered under his breath, "You'll see. I'm a better man."

"There's nothing left for you to show me, my daughter is dead.

We're entering the city - Where can I drop you off."

Geremy points to the curb and Mr. Olswain pulls over and lets him out. He was barely out of the car and Mr. Olswain pulled away to catch up with Harry's car and continued following it to the funeral home. Once out of the vehicle, they said a prayer, asking for the strength to bear what was to follow.

No one asked where was Geremy.

Chapter 7:
Family Bonding

The funeral home was quite large, as city places go, the Director greeted them and offered his condolences. He escorted them into the viewing room and instructed them to take as much time as needed.

Angelica laid there on the steel table; a blanket coveted her cold body. You could see bruising about her head and neck. Not in their wildest of dreams had the Olswains ever thought that they would be looking down at their daughter in this place.

When you become a parent, your future is modified to include the provisional nurturing, care, education, and moral structure needed to raise children. But when a parent loses their only child, their future days are darkened much more, with an irreplaceable loss of dreams and hopes. This instantaneous darkness covered the Olswain's that evening when they were first told, sending a father to search an empty car and throwing a mother down to her knees from the incredible weight of emptiness.

Yet, standing before that cold steel table, that now supported Angelica, the pain of their loss was lessened by the hope of new life.

They remained there for a while talking to Angelica, remembering good times and bad, confessing to her about times when they misjudged her. They ended this visit with the promise that they would take care of her child.

Harry followed into the room after them. There was a glass window that looked into the room. As he approached her body, his tears drenched his face, and he fell to his knees. Mr. Olswain, having watched this through the window, rushed into the room and helped him to stand to his feet. Trembling with the lost and a feeling that he had never before felt, he thanked Mr. Olswain. Harry reached into his pocket and placed their wedding rings back on Angelica's finger and repeated the vows that he wrote for her at their wedding.

> *"To my lover, my friend, and my soulmate. I have loved you from the first time your eyes met mine, your strength met my strength and your heart*

filled mine. Where there was darkness, you brought the light. Where there was emptiness, you filled with joy and where there was loneliness you filled with your image. I will continue to love you long past the time that our eyes can no longer see, our hands can no longer reach, and our ears can no longer hear because I am bonded to you beyond earthly ties."

They left the room together, and the three of them hugged as a family at the door. The funeral director approached and let them know that he had spoken with Charlie. The body will be driven to his funeral home later today.

Harry suggested, "let's go have some lunch, and I will show you where we called home."

Their home was not in the luxurious hi-rise condo that Geremy often waited to stalk Angelica hoping to see her enter and depart. Harry and Angelica purchased a house just outside of the city before their wedding, a place that they could build on as they strengthened their lives together. As you walked into the house, Angelica and Harry's wedding picture was hanging on the wall to the left.

Beneath the picture was a curio that held the same family portrait hanging on the left foyer wall in the Olswain's house. Harry did not have any similar photos because he was orphaned as an infant. The child of single child parents, there were no next of kin to find. So, he was placed with wonderful foster parents who decided to return him back into the system at the age of 5, to pursue a different life. From there, it was the usual story — getting bounced around until the age of 18. He became a firefighter because his records revealed how his parents died in a fatal crash, and he wanted to be able to save lives and prevent other children from a parentless childhood. They continued their tour of this 4-bedroom 4000 sq.-ft home. The Olswain's were pleased to see that their daughter had not only found happiness in Harry but that she also lived in joy.

It was around 3 o'clock that afternoon that they received the phone call.

Dr. Sharindha, "Hello Harry, I have some news for you, can you come down to the center."

"We will leave right now."

"We?"

"Yes, I have Angelica's parents with me."

"Good, I look forward to meeting them."

Excitement filled the house. They rushed to Harry's car.

Mr. Olswain, "If she is telling us to come down, it must be good news! …right?"

Harry, "She did not sound like she had disappointing news."

Macie," We will all know when we get there, how long will it take to get there, Harry?"

"30 minutes."

They remained in silence for the entire drive, each having their own thoughts, dreams, and expectations.

When they arrived at the Center, they each took in a deep breath and exhaled. They looked at each other and were ready. Dr. Sharindha was waiting at the door, she tried to hide her emotions, but she did not have a good poker face. Her excitement was just as emotional as Harry's.

"Come-in, Come-in, it's very nice to meet you, I've heard so much about you from Angelica. Please go down the hall to the first patient room."

The room was decorated with custom labeled balloons and streamers. The label on the balloons read "Happy Zygote Day." Margarite was lying in bed under the decorations. As they walked into the room, she yelled, "Surprise!! were pregnant". Joy filled the room and hugs all around.

"Hello Margarite, I'm the child your carrying's Grandmother, Macie, Thank you."

"and I'm the Grandfather, Peter, it's a pleasure to meet you."

Harry held Margarite's hand and said to her, "You are the hope of this family, and that makes you family. Thank you"

Dr. Sharindha and her staff pushed a cart down the hall, leaving it outside the room, carrying a cake and glasses of ginger ale, a party pursued. Margarite will have to remain in the Center for the weekend to complete a limited mobility period.

Macie asked, "So, Margarite how often have you done this?"

"This is my first time."

"How old are you, my dear."

"30"

"How many children do you have."

"one, I gave birth to her when I was 16 and gave her up for adoption."

"Are you married?"

"no"

"Where do you live?"

"I live with my brother and his fiancée in their condo."

"you are carrying my grandchild; I would love for you to come and live with us."

"I thought I would live in Harry's house."

Like Mr. Olswain, Macie too had a knack of getting straight to the point and sleuthing answers. It's known that when people stay together long enough they start to become one thought. Well, the Olswains had sleuthing down to a science.

"Really, how do you know Harry?"

"a year ago, he saved my life. I was camping and got trapped in the 'campfire' fires. Harry came through the flames and rescued me. I never saw him again after that but thought about him often. The day that I was turning in my surrogate agreement at the center was the day he came in with his wife. "

"So, your hope, is that over the next 9 months, the two of you would spend time together. And then what, fall in love? I don't know if that will happen or not happen. In either case, I will not stand in the way of love, my daughter is no longer here, and Harry deserves to find happiness again when he is ready. What I do know is that the child you carry inside of you is the most essential thing in my life. Please, come, live with us. "

The two-woman starred into each other's eyes in silence one in confusion and the other with determination. Macie sensed Margarite's growing tension, smiled and said, "rest on it. I will return tomorrow. Are you on a restricted diet, or can I bring you breakfast"?

"No restrictions. "

"Good, now tell me what it is you like, and I will bring it tomorrow, and I will keep this conversation between you and me."

Macie fixes Margarite's hair about her forehead and down her face, "See you in the morning." Macie leaves the bedside and walks into the hall "Alright gentlemen, let's leave so she can rest. Doctor, too you and your staff...Thank you very much. I will return in the morning."

Macie returned for a few hours every morning, afternoon, and evening leading up to Monday. Margarite talked about her childhood, battles with her parents, the birth of a child at the age of 16 while Macie did the same telling stories about Angelica and her love for a young man in grade school, without revealing any names. Macie also shared some stories about her life, her life with her parents, and her life with Peter.

Macie was under the notion that if we were going to live together, we should do so, as a family. The more we could share, the stronger the bond– the family bond. Peter and Harry were also bonding, they would visit with Margarite individually twice a day sharing childhood and adult stories. This was the Macie plan to build family unity. Macie also stated that it is good for the baby to hear the voice of his or her father. During Margarite's private times with Harry, she never mentioned the story she shared with Macie.

Monday morning had finally arrived, and to the surprise of everyone, except for Margarite and the Center staff, there were additional members to the party. Margarite's brother and soon to be sister-in-law. Her brother was not very keen on the whole idea of her becoming a surrogate mother but thought that they would have more time to discuss it. Only to find out that the same day that she joined she was matched to a family. Then 3-days after that to find out that this family wants to take you from the city to live with them.

Her brother spoke, "Hello I am Margarite's brother Carl, and this is my fiancée, Stacy…", The usual returned greetings followed, "I will tell you when Margarite first talked to me about becoming a surrogate I was doubtful and then to say that she was leaving to live with you, I was not onboard. But when she shared with me (us) your commitment to having a true family bond it brought a feeling of trust. So, if you do not mind, we would like to follow you to your home, so I can physically see where my sister will be residing."

Macie responded, "I am so pleased to hear and see your concern for your sister, by all means, you are welcome."

Margarite asked, "How do you intend to follow us. You city dwellers don't believe in owning cars."

"Oh, I forgot to mention, there will be one more person joining us, a longtime friend and co-worker. Let me bring him in and introduce you."

Carl walked outside and gestured for his friend to leave the car and come in.

"Everyone, this is my friend, Geremy."

Harry was quick to speak, "We know Geremy. He grew up next door to the Olswains and was Angelica's, first love. He was also with Angelica on the train when she died."

Carl, "I did not know that. If this is uncomfortable, could we ride there with you, and we can take public transportation back."

Peter looks at Geremy "no worries, let's stay on plan."

They all exit the Center and head in their cars to the Olswain's house.

After returning to the car Carl says to Geremy, "None of this fit's right in my head. You were in a train accident where your childhood love dies, you met her secret husband and took him to meet her parents, and you knew about the surrogate situation, yet on the way here you said nothing because you didn't think it would be the same family. Either you think I'm stupid, or you are. Don't lie to me, Geremy, what's going on here?"

Geremy in anger, "You don't think that there are things in my life that I want to keep to myself. News Flash Carl! — I don't share everything with you. Having her die on that train broke me into pieces and to learn that she was married. What was wrong with me, why could she not love me!!! I've always been here, why didn't she tell me."

"Tell you what?"

"why didn't she tell me that she was married."

Carl looked at Stacy in the back seat with confusion. What is going on in Geremy's mind? He's been out of this girl's life since High School, yet he speaks of their love as if they were never apart. Did being there on that train as Angelica died, place him into some kind of psychotic delusion. Carl was determined that his friend needed some help, but at this moment he was more concerned with his sister's safety. There wasn't much conversation during the rest of the trip.

Margarite rode with Harry, with all of the sharing over the weekend there was not much to talk about. Margarite asked him, "have you given any thought to whether the baby will be a boy or girl."

59

Harry shrugged his shoulders and said, "No, with everything leading up to today I have not."

"I realize that this is very hard for you, When Macie asked me to live with them, I told her that I thought I would live with you. You know, this way, you would not have to be alone, and you could see your child grow each day."

"Wow... That sounds terrific, but I think this way is better. Macie will know what to do if you need help."

"you're probably right. Will you be visiting often?"

"Macie said it would be good for the child to hear my voice. So, I will be here as often as I can, and I just want to thank you again for doing this for us."

Margarite smiles. She knows it's too soon to discuss her feelings for Harry. After all his wife hasn't been placed into the ground yet. They drove a little further, and Harry said, "I'm glad that your family is with us. Going to live with a family you don't know must have you a little worried."

"I am, but they seem to be very nice. Is that the same feeling that you have?"

"I do, I've only known them for 4-days. I feel very comfortable around them. They truly loved their daughter."

"Macie told me the story of how you were secretly married, and this was the first time meeting you. I hope they don't hold me to their daughter's standards, I did not know her, but I am quite sure that we will be different."

Harry laughed "No worries, I won't drop you off and run away. I will be here until after we've buried Angelica."

Margarite looked at him and smiled again.

Meanwhile, the conversation in the Olswains car started a little differently, "What a surprise to see Geremy show up. Do you know on our drive down Geremy had the audacity, to be mad at Angelica because she married Harry and not him? What an asshole—here he had the prize in his grasp and did not act. And because of his inabilities to do so, he thinks my daughter is to blame. I should have brought Carl and Stacy here in my car and told Geremy to go to Hell."

"Easy, Peter, take a breath. I, too, was very set back by his presence and it appeared Carl was also taken by surprise. To think that Geremy did not tell him that he knew us."

"That boys head is not on straight. I am so happy that Angelica did not marry him and to think I thought he would be the best candidate."

"Candidate? Like you would have had a choice in the matters of the heart."

"your right."

The journey home finally ended, and everyone starts to get out of the cars. Mr. Olswain walks over to Geremy's car and says to Geremy, "Perhaps you may want to take this time to check on your parent's house. We will call you when we are done."

Geremy nods his head and tells Carl to call him when they are ready.

As they walked into the house, Stacy states that their home is beautiful. Margarite, having never viewed Angelica, looked at the family portrait and said, "What a lovely picture, Angelica is beautiful."

"Thank you", Macie grabs Margarite's hand, "… and I hope you find the same joy here that she found."

Peter continues the tour starting upstairs and working their way back to the kitchen. Once in the kitchen, Margarite walked over and sat down on the round window box seat, the way Angelica always sat in it. The Olswains looked at each other and smiled.

Peter "Margarite, welcome to our home."

Carl walked over to his sister, kissed her on the head and whispered to her, "are you good here, say the word, and I will take you back with me."

Margarite smiles at Carl and looks to the Olswains "I think" as she nestles her lower abdominal area "... we will be happy here."

Macie yells out with excitement, "Thank You. It's been a long ride, there is a lovely restaurant down the road that delivers, are you hungry."

Carl says, "we would love to, but we should grab Geremy and head back."

"Nonsense," says Peter, "Call Geremy and tell him we are going to have dinner here, what does he want from Antoine's?"

The Olswains must have ordered everything on the menu. The amount of food that came in the door was far greater than the breakfast that Macie prepared a couple of mornings before. The group was stuffed and content. Margarite was the first to say it "Macie, I'm starting to get a little sleepy, which room is for me." Macie's first thought was to place her into Angelica's room, but just as she planned everything else, she knew that this was not Angelica and that she would probably appreciate being treated as Margarite. "Please take the room at the end of the hall, my dear."

Margarite turns to her brother, and they exchange a hug as though they would never see each other again. She whispers in his ear, "don't worry, I will be all right", then she embraced Stacy.

Macie looks on and extends an invitation to Carl, "Mi Casa Su Casa, come anytime to visit your sister."

Carl smiled and looked to Geremy, "Let's go."

Geremy stood in a position where his direct eye contact was on Margarite and said, "Good night."

Chapter 8:
The Pregnancy

The next morning Carl mentioned Geremy's strange behavior to Dave. "What do you think of it," asked Carl. "Freaky, Let's keep our eyes on him. Maybe it was a flashback to when he was experimenting with the dark sexuality side of himself."

That following weekend Angelica was finally laid to rest. Her tombstone was shaped like the curved kitchen window seat with a small angel sitting in the middle. Above the angel's head read, "To my lover, my friend, and my soulmate. Forever Bonded"

The service was well attended with family and friends. Carl and Stacy were among the attendees, as well as Geremy who drove them there. This time they stayed at Geremy's parents' house. Geremy had reopened the house so they would have a place to stay when visiting and not have to feel as though they were intruding.

Over the coming months, the three made several visits, in fact, the Olswains started feeling better about Geremy again due to his dedication to a friend.

Margarite would have occasional stayover's at Geremy's parents' house when her brother was visiting. Geremy was strengthening his bond with Margarite as she started looking towards him as an extended family member.

Harry made several visits. He and Margarite would take long walks together to ensure that she was getting her exercise. He would tell her tales of the city while she would talk about trips into the small town and the looks people would give her. It would seem that many of the villagers knew she was carrying Angelica's baby. The time with Harry brought Margarite the most joy.

As they entered the second trimester, the baby's motion became more prevalent, and the baby bump was now a baby pouch. She enjoyed having Harry place his hand on her belly and feel the movement as he would talk to the baby. Harry elected not to know the sex of the child, he said in the discussions that he and Angelica would have on children that was something they both agreed on.

Margarite's bond with Stacy also strengthened during their visits, she was no longer the girl my brother was going to marry, they were becoming sisters. She shared with Stacy the Harry Fireman story and asked that it stay between them. A trust was formed. She shared with her the excitement from their walks together and the intimate way that she would feel when he touched her. Stacy thought that it was good to allow her to indulge in her joy but in a sisterly way she pointed out that these are only your dreams at the moment, Harry quite naturally enjoys your company, but at this moment his genuine compassion and love is to the child.

As old houses go sounds are sometimes heard through the walls or the vents. When the two would talk during sleepovers, Harry would leave Carl watching a sporting event and go to the basement. There he would lift the cover off of the vent and listen to the conversations in the sleepover room. Geremy's anger increased hearing the fireman story. Not again, he thought. First, you took Angelica from me, and now the woman carrying my child is in love with you as well. This must change.

Over the next sleepovers, Geremy said to Margarite that he read somewhere that expecting mothers should get plenty of exercise and asked if they could go on walks. She saw nothing wrong in his request and thought it was a good idea. The town was small, so, they often times traveled in the same areas where Harry and Margarite would walk, Geremy would strut like a peacock, the proud father, which was completely different from Harry's walk. He would look villagers in the face and smile to ensure that they noticed the two of them. He would think to himself — wait until you people see that I am the real father then You'll be greeting me with cigars and well wishes. Geremy built a story in his mind of joyful times with Angelica with a loving relationship that led to the ultimate joy of a child.

This continued, and now we are in the third trimester the home stretch. Geremy's walks diminished because Harry was living at the house full time. He took a leave of absence so that he could be there to rush her to the hospital. It was decided that the baby would be born in a Hospital and not the fertility center. This did not please Geremy, and every weekend, he would ask Carl, "Are you going to visit Margarite this weekend." Carl's response was even less pleasing "No, Harry is going to be there, and he will call me when it's time. Thank you for all these weeks of allowing me to share your home" they clasp hands and hug "True buds."

Geremy responded, "Buds to the end."

Margarite reached a state of ultimate bliss; Harry was all hers she thought, he took a leave of absence to stay with me, each morning when I wake, he will be here. Please, baby, don't come early.

Carl was getting fed up of Geremy's constant request on the baby's arrival. He thought Geremy was acting like he's the expecting father, what gives with this guy.

Between Geremy and Margarite having misplaced joy, Carl and Stacy had their hands full trying to make sense of it all and then the call came.

It was 2:00 am on a Friday that Carl received the call from Harry, "we're on our way to the hospital." Carl and Harry also created a great bond during this time. Carl said, "great, we will rent a car and come right away."

Harry responded, "I got you. My captain is going to pick up you and Stacy and bring you to the border of the city where you will transfer to another captain and so on until you are here. Get moving, he will be at your door very soon."

Carl and Stacy got dressed, threw a bag together, and were escorted through the areas with sirens blaring.

Harry arrived at the hospital at 2:15 am, and the baby was born with no complications at 6:30 am. Margarite asked Harry to stay with her during the birthing. He and Macie had attended Lamar's training classes. It was a beautiful baby boy, 7-lbs 8-oz. Margarite was a great surrogate mother and in excellent health also. Harry placed a kiss on her cheek and thanked her. He named the child, Peter, after Angelica's dad.

Macie had constructed a plan that completely bonded two families together for the safety and wellbeing of her grandchild. She had deliberately not discussed the post-birthing outcome. Although Macie had built an incredible bond with Margarite, almost loved her as a daughter, Macie now had her grandson in her arms and Margarites services were over. She wanted to raise her grandson with the image of only Angelica.

Dr. Sharindha and the surrogate mother team were there to assist in the separation process (surrogate mother and child). At this time the Baby and the Intended Parents are separated from the surrogate mother. Both families were aware that this would be coming. This is why Harry made the necessary arrangements to get Carl and Stacy there quickly. He felt Margarite's feelings for him growing stronger with each passing day and had discussed it with Carl. He told Carl that he had no intention of hurting or leading his sister on. During this time, I am only focused on the birthing of my child. Carl understood what Harry was saying and the emotional state that it was coming from.

Margarite was having a tough time, the emotional state that she placed herself into could only lead to massive disappointment. She exclaimed, "How can they just walk away like that, I thought we were family. They used me and did not care about me, Harry and I were connecting, I know he likes me."

The surrogate counselors were trying to combat the feeling of abandonment by reminding her of the reality of surrogate pregnancy. Our purpose is to help families that cannot bring children into the world a path for fulfillment.

Stacy was in the corner of the room in tears for the hurt that Margarite was feeling. She was asking herself should I have been more forceful and not allow her to live in the fantasy world that she created. Look at what it has done to her and can Margarite ever recover. Fraught with guilt and sadness, she fled the room to get Carl. Carl entered the room and was shocked by the display his sister was giving.

"Please, everyone can you let me have a minute with my sister, alone."

"Margarite, this is what we talked about. When we read the pamphlet on surrogate pregnancy, it strongly stressed the emotional effect of turning the child over to the intended parents. I told you that I could not see you being able to do it. Now here we are ... and you are doing what you said you would not do. How do we move on from here?"

"I don't know, I didn't think it would hurt this bad. I feel so torn. It's not like when I was 16 a child having a child. I wanted this child to be so perfect, and he is, I did that! They made me feel like a real part of the family, now they want me to go away. Is this how my child felt, being abandoned by her mother. I've never thought about her since then until right now. How could I birth another child that I cannot raise?"

"And that's all you did. This was not one of your eggs, fertilized by someone you loved. This was you renting your womb to birth another woman's egg, fertilized by a man who loved her. You did something fantastic here, and I am so proud of you, but sister, I need you to understand this is different. This child is with his rightful family. This child is home, and you made it possible. You were his first responder, his fireman carrying him to safety. Now you need to rest, Stacy and I will be here with you."

Carl sat in the chair next to his sister, holding her hand. Stacy peeks into the room and tells the others that they can come back in. They stayed only a few minutes and left. Stacy sat in the chair at the end of the bed. There they sat quietly in their own thoughts, shortly falling to sleep.

They were awakened at 1:00 pm by a knocking at the door. In walked a series of servers with carts of food for their lunch and a large heart-shaped red rose arrangement. The server gave an envelope to Margarite, inside was a beautiful thank you card and a note.

My dearest Margarite, The Olswain and Albert family cannot thank you enough for helping our families to enjoy the gift that our daughter Angelica wanted to leave for us. You will be remembered and forever be in our thoughts each time we look at our Son / Grandson. —Thank you.

Margarite read the note and handed it to Carl, saying, "This is what family does. I was their first responder." She reflected back to the way she felt when Harry saved her and was becoming satisfied with having returned the favor. A life for a life.

Chapter 9:
The Wedding

Carl took the following two weeks off from work to spend it with his sister and her recovery process. The entire experience revealed a lot of emotion that Margarite did not realize was in her from giving up a child at sixteen. She and Carl would spend hours jogging, running, and talking together. They became a stronger family unit with Margarite accepting Stacy as her big sister helping to plan the wedding together. And although Margarite was very comfortable welcoming surrogacy as a first responder for parents needing help to bring their special little package to life, she did not do it again.

Her feelings for Harry still lingered, but she managed to place them on the side for now. The words that continually rang in her head were from Macie when she said, "Harry needs to find happiness again when he is ready." Margarite wanted to make sure she would be around when that time comes. For now, helping with the wedding and finding a new career was keeping her busy.

The wedding date is set, and the location will be magical.

Although Carl and Geremy had a difference of understanding during the Angelica ordeal, they were still friends. As friends, Carl always wanted Geremy by his side, as his best man.

It was at the wedding that Geremy and Margarite reconnected for the first time. Geremy wanted to know about the child, his perceived offspring. Geremy could not ask Carl what the outcome of the birth was. Carl had closed that door to any future conversations. So now at the wedding, it was his chance to speak with Margarite.

Geremy managed to get Margarite alone,

"Margarite, it's nice to see you again, I've missed our walks."

Margarite replied, "That seems so long ago."

"So, what did you have, a boy or a girl."

"I really do not want to talk about that."

"Just help me to close the loop, she was my friend, boy, or girl."

"Fine, it was a boy."

"Nice! what name did they give him."

"Seriously, I'm going back to the party, you need to get over this"

When Margarite returned to the room, her brother was looking for her.

"There you are! It's my turn to dance with you. Where have you been".

Margarite knew this was her brother's day and would not allow for anything to disrupt it, so she did not mention the conversation she just had with Geremy. The wedding continued with no further incidents.

The flight home found Geremy and Margarite together again. He apologized for his questioning and asked if he could repair the damage with dinner when the plane lands. Margarite accepted his offer as being a sincere effort to apologize. They continued the flight with idle chatter and times of rested silence. The flight attendant makes the proper landing announcements, and they land safely.

They debarked and proceeded to Geremy's car in the parking lot. During the short drive to a nearby restaurant, the conversations remained upbeat and relaxed. After dinner, he offered to drive Margarite home. When they arrived at the car, Geremy pointed out, "I had a great evening, are you still staying at Carl's house."

"No, I moved out last week. I live in the Capital Park area now. "

They set a course to her apartment, and Geremy asked where she was working. As a young woman growing up, Margarite had always been told that she was top model material. Using what God gave her, she contacted CASTIMAGES a model & talent agency and landed a job with one of the local fashion designers. She was so excited as she laid out all the details of getting the job and the runway trips coming up. Geremy shared with her excitement and let her know that he would like to continue their friendship. They agreed and set plans to meet in the mornings for runs in the park and coffee. This continued for several months with occasional dinners and movies. Geremy also attended some of her runway tours. Carl was aware of the friendship and hoped that it would only stay as friends.

Margarites career was taking off, and she was featured on the local style television show which was then highlighted on the local news to promote the upcoming fashion week event. The next morning Geremy told Margarite that he saw her on the news. In his mind, he thought this would be an excellent time to ask if they could move their relationship beyond friends until she asked the question, "do you think Harry may have seen the fashion news article."

"What? Harry, who?"

"Harry Albert"

"FIREMAN Harry?"

Geremy turns away from Margarite. He could not believe that history was going to repeat itself. Harry took away Angelica, he's got my son and now he's on the verge of taking away Margarite. Not this time. This time I will tell the girl how I feel. This time it's going to be different, once I tell her she'll forget about fireman Harry and be mine. As he turns around Margarite is walking into her building she waves with a "Good Night"

The next morning Geremy waited at the meet-up point but no Margarite. Margarite was called out of the country for a model shoot. Geremy, not knowing why she was not there, twisted the whole thing around his jealous thoughts. In his mind, Harry saw the news and contacted Margarite, right now the two of them are together. He lost again and wanted to do something to hurt Harry, Geremy thought if Margarite knew that he was the father she would want to keep the family together thus bringing hurt to Harry. Now he needed to find Margarite.

Chapter 10:
Peter's Birthday

Harry was enjoying fatherhood, and Peter was now approaching a year. He stayed with the Olswain's for the first month learning how to care for a young child. Harry wanted to take Peter back home and be the father that Angelica had always told him he would become, it wasn't easy to leave the Olswain's, Macie was very disappointed. She pointed out that with the type of job he had, how could he dedicate the proper amount of time for a child. Harry knew that this day would come and had applied for a desk/training position at the fire department and set up nursery care at a local daycare. This was a daycare that he and Angelica would always pass on their way home. He remembered Angelica saying that it would be a convenient place for when they would decide to have children.

Approaching his 1st year, Macie wants to throw Peter's 1st birthday party. Harry agreed but insisted that it take place at his house.

!!! Party time Come and Join us at Peter's 1-year Birthday Party!!!

The room was filled with his daycare friends and their parents, The Olswain's and their family, friends, firemen, and neighbors. Peter was having a great time with presents and toys, cake and ice cream. Also invited to the party, Carl and Stacy.

The doorbell rang, and Macie answered the door, surprised to see Carl and Stacy standing there. They both embraced her and greeted her with smiles. Harry, not having any family continued their bond of friendship started by Macie's Plan. They walked in and scooped Peter up, it was apparent to Macie that this was not their first-time meeting Peter. Carl, while holding Peter high over his head, said, "Happy Birthday Peter, are you happy to see your Uncle Carl and look, Aunt Stacy is here too." Macie walked over to Harry, "Uncle and Aunt, what's going on." He explained that they kept in contact with each other and formed a true friendship. At this moment, Carl and Stacy walked up and joined the conversation, "Macie is Peter senior with you."

"Yes, he just ran out to get something from the store."

Stacy uttered, "I could tell at the door that this is a complete surprise for you, but these two are like brothers."

"Well Yes, I am shocked, I don't know what to think, but looking at all of your faces, I feel happy."

"and that's how we feel, even more so — now that you know."

"and Margarite, is she going to be walking in next."

Carl replied, "No. Margarite has no knowledge that Harry, and I continuing our friendship. It's too soon."

"I think about her often, and I've been following her modeling career. She's established quite a name for herself. I've thought several times to reach out to her, to tell her how special she is".

"I know that Margarite would like to hear that from you, someday."

"When she is ready, you let me know."

"She's much stronger than the last time you saw her. Perhaps on Peter's 2nd Birthday, we could have a reunion of sorts."

"That would be Great. I will place it on the calendar."

Margarite had not forgotten that one year ago, she gave birth to a child.

Rumors around the fashion network say that Margarite went to a nearby orphanage that catered to children from ages infancy to 5 years and threw a party for all of the one-year-olds.

!!Happy Birthday, Peter"

Chapter 11:
Moving Forward

Margarite was away for three months and returned with exciting news, she was selected to be in a movie. She was to have a non-speaking role as an extra in a large cast. Her agent said that she would be in many scenes, including a possible close-up. She would need to leave for filming in one month, and it is anticipated to take a year to produce. She had to sign an agreement that forbade her from discussing the content and the title.

She called Carl during her travels home and broke the news. He and Stacy were very happy for her.

"My little sister in the movies. I cannot wait to see it."

"it is going to take a year before its release so calm down. Don't go off telling people about it yet."

"OK, OK, what time do you get in maybe we can get some dinner.

"Sounds great, I get in at 4:45pm."

He made reservations at her favorite restaurant. As she stepped out of the terminal, she was bombarded by the fashion paparazzi. Carl opened the car door, and she quickly jumped in. He placed her bags in the trunk.

"Wow, paparazzi!! Your trip must have gone quite well."

"It was amazing. Top designers, Top models, Beautiful sets, and I was invited to be there. This is well beyond my dreams. Where are we eating, I'm starving?"

"now it's my turn to say calm down, you'll see."

"Wait, this doesn't look like a rental car?"

"It's not. Surprised that we city dwellers can buy cars?"

As they pull up to the restaurant, Margarite smiled, "you must have really missed me, or do you guys have something to tell me."

"yes, I do have something to share, but by the tone of your voice, it's not what you think. Let's get in and get our table."

They were seated by the window and placed their orders.

"So, what is the news you want to share, I assume, is not that I'm going to be an aunt."

"Oh no! it's not that", says Stacy, "although we are starting to discuss it."

Margarite Smiles.

"I received a promotion. A big promotion. You are now looking at the Senior Vice President of all West Coast Operations, which also includes Hawaii."

"Oh my God, that's enormous. Congratulation!! I assume that it comes with an impressive salary?"

"Spectacular"

Margarite raises her glass, "Cheers." Glasses clinked together, and conversations continued.

Carl drops Margarite home, and Stacy gives her a hug "Goodnight." Unknown to them at the time as they drove off there was a parked car with someone sitting inside, it was Geremy.

Geremy was stalking her apartment in the manner that he was stalking Angelica's. He was pleased to see that she was dropped off by her brother, and he left shortly after.

The next day Margarite started her usual daily schedule and who should she meet on her run but Geremy.

"Hello Margarite"

"Hello, Geremy, good to see you."

"Yes, where have you been."

"I was in Europe doing an amazing model shoot. I met so many influential people in the fashion industry. "

"Oh, you were in Europe. I did not know what to think, I thought maybe you had gotten married."

"Married??, who would I have married. Geremy I run and jog with you. My life is so fragmented—no time for a sex life or to go places to meet anyone."

"Ghee, you make me feel like chop liver. The only worth I bring to you is a run and jog."

"Geremy, you're my brothers' friend, and I consider you as a second brother."

Geremy listened to her words as they tore through his soul. A second brother! He was tired of being the third wheel, the afterthought. His relationship with Carl was starting to weaken, Stacy took care of that. He was spending more time alone than before. He did not want to be her second brother; you gave birth to my child, and it's time that you knew it. When we stop for coffee, I'm going to tell her.

Ring... Ring ...ring. It was Margarite's phone.

"Geremy, I'm sorry, but I have to get home, my agent just sent a limousine to pick me up and take me to a meeting. I have to cut our run short, no time for coffee today".

Margarite ran off to her home, leaving Geremy in the park. He stood there fuming over what transpired getting hotter every second as if Hell was boiling over. But there was nothing else that he could do today, so he turned and went back towards his car.

Margarite did not get a call, from her agent, it was a telemarketer trying to sell life insurance. She did not like the tone Geremy took when she referred to him as a second brother. His facial expression reflected genuine hurt and disgust. Margarite wanted to talk to Carl about it. After arriving home and carefully thinking about Geremy's behavior, she placed a call to her brother and was unable to reach him, she left a message. A half an hour went by, and she sent him a text. An hour after that she texted Stacy, I've been trying to reach Carl, do you know where he is. Stacy texted back, He's on a plane to Hawaii. Can I help you? Margarite paused, thinking if she wanted to bring Stacy in on this mess. She replied, it's about Geremy. Stacy texted back, let's meet for lunch at the Deli near the office.

Margarite arrived at the Deli at 11:45am and got a table. Stacy joined her at Noon. "Stacy, thank you for joining me."

"What's going on with you and Geremy?"

"It's nothing like that, at least not for me. Geremy and I have met to run and jog in the mornings since we returned back for your wedding. While I was out running this morning, we ran back into each other. He questioned me about where I've been and when I told him. He said that he thought that I had run off and got married. Then he expressed that he was interested in me, and I told him that I look at him as a second brother. The look on his face and the tone in which he responded scared me. I wanted Carl to know."

"Carl will arrive at the airport in Hawaii by 4pm. Send a text now, saying I need to talk to you about Geremy's behavior. He will respond as soon as he gets it."

"Is there a history here that I don't know about, they've had a long friendship."

"I will leave that talk to you and your brother. I have to get back to work, Bye!"

"Bye"

Margarite had hoped that her worries would go away after speaking with Stacy; instead, her fears increased. She decided to stay away from Geremy until she heard from her brother. This was going to be a long day. Geremy has already called twice. On the second attempt, he left a message apologizing for his rudeness and offering a makeup dinner tonight after work. The time difference between Sacramento, CA and Hawaii is 2 hours, which means the soonest Margarite could hear from Carl would be 6pm her time. She knew Geremy would call her at 5pm and continue calling until she picked up. He knows where I live, and if he can't reach me by phone, he may come knocking at my door. I don't want to leave my place, but I could go over to my brother's house with Stacy. What time is it 3:30, let me call her?

"Hello"

"Stacy, it's me, Margarite."

"Well if you're calling me at work, something must have changed, what's wrong."

"Geremy called and left a message he wants to go to dinner tonight. I haven't spoken to him. I'm afraid if I don't respond, he might come to my house. Can I stay with you?"

"Sure, we haven't changed the locks. Do you still have your key?"

"I do. I'm going to head there now. Thank you!"

Margarite arrived at the house at 4pm. Geremy called again at 4:30 and left a message that he would pick her up at 5:30pm. Carl's plane arrived in Hawaii early, and he read Margarite's text as he was departing the aircraft. He called her immediately, and she explained the situation. He used a few explicative comments and said he would take care of it. Then he asked her to put Stacy on the line.

"Stacy isn't home from work yet."

"Stacy gets home at 4pm. Margarite, go to the kitchen and see if the key to your place is on the key holders by the door."

"There aren't any keys on the hooks."

When Margarite moved into her place, she gave Carl a spare key for emergencies.

"Damn it!"

"What"

"Stacy is at your house. She's going to confront Geremy."

"Should I rush over there."

"No, Geremy is not that crazy, and Stacy can handle herself. Let her do her thing."

Geremy arrived at Margarites house at 5:30 and rang the doorbell. The door opened, and there stood Stacy.

"What are you doing here. Where is Margarite?"

"Away from you. This is Carl's sister you're messing with, have you no sense of loyalty and respect... But then I already know the answer to that question. Remember, on my second day at the firm you asked me out to dinner, and nothing happened after that. I never returned any of your phone calls nor accepted any of your invites. It was because I saw you, yeah, I saw you parked in my buildings parking lot that next morning and then again that evening. You were stalking me. "

"That's absurd. You're making this up because I lost interest in you."

"I'm not here to debate with you, leave Margarite alone."

Geremy raised his hands in a simple conversational gesture that Stacy misunderstood for aggression and pulled a Taser from her pocket.

"I will use this, step back."

"Whoa!! I would never hurt you or anybody else."

"Leave Margarite alone."

"Done! I'm going to back up and leave."

Geremy left the building, and Stacy checked the parking lot and the surrounding area for his car an return home. She let out a sigh of relief and started laughing as she remembered the look on his face when he saw the Taser. Ring...ring... Ring

"Hey, Babe, are you OK."

"Carl, yes, I'm fine. Did you talk to your sister?"

"yes, I did, and when she told me that you were not home and the key to her apartment was missing, I knew where you were. How did it go?"

"I think he got the message to leave her alone, but he still needs to hear it from you."

"Oh, without a doubt, he will hear it from me, I'd rather do it when we are face to face."

"I agree. We are good for now. The shock on Geremy's face when he saw my Taser was priceless."

"Your Taser!!!, Wow it went that far."

"We can talk when you get back."

Stacy never told Carl about Geremy because of their close friendship. Now it's time to let it out of the closet. Stacy returned home, and when she walked inside, she was greeted with a very tight hug and kiss on the cheek.

"Are you alright, did you really go to my apartment and talk to Geremy."

"Yeah"

"You're a real kick-ass older sister. What did you say? How did he take it?"

"Well, when I opened the door, he was stunned and confused, asking me where you were. He didn't even say, Hello."

"Oh, you really shook him up."

"I told him, you wanted to be far away from him and that he should keep it that way. I said you are Carl's best friend, and this is his sister, where's your sense of respect."

"Weren't you afraid he might attack you."

"This guy's afraid of his own shadow besides I had my equalizer with me."

Carl had given Stacy the Taser when he took the new job role. He knew he would be traveling and wanted her to feel safe when he was gone.

"you have a gun."

"No, No. Carl gave me this heavy-duty multiple shot Taser. I pulled it out at the end of our conversation because he did not look like he was going to leave. His eyes extended, and he could barely talk, he was so scared, then he backed up and left."

"I wish I could have seen that. Thank you, Thank you."

"why don't you stay with me here until Carl comes back at the end of the week. I'll take an early lunch tomorrow, and we can swing by your place to get a few things while Geremy is at work."

"That sounds Great, I could use a little Sister time."

They talked all through the night.

Chapter 12:
The Truth

Stacy was so tired the next day that she did not notice the bold attempts that Geremy was making to avoid any interaction with her. Geremy noticed Stacy had left early and to him, that could only mean that she was meeting Margarite. He went back to his office and sat down; his rage was evident. Then Geremy took out some letter size stationary and wrote something down. He sealed it into a manila envelope and with his black marker wrote 'THE TRUTH' on the face of it. He waited until everyone in the office stepped out for lunch, then grabbed his envelope keeping the words THE TRUTH concealed against his side and walked into Stacy's office, leaving it on her chair.

Geremy did not take his usual lunch break, he elected to take a late lunch after Stacy returned to the office. Stacy came back and found the envelope. The envelope was not addressed to anyone, so as she picked it up, she scanned the halls with her eyes to see if anyone was watching her read it. She carefully cut back the top and pulled out the letter. It read, 'You cannot keep me away from the woman that gave birth to my child. That's right, here's the Truth. THE BABY IS MINE!! Signed Geremy.

Stacy's knees weakened just from the thought of what if this is true, as she sat in her chair, thinking. The heartbreak for Harry to find out Angelica committed an act of infidelity; Margarite whose thoughts are still on Harry to know that Geremy wants her as the baby's birth mother; then the shock of disappointment to the Olswain's of their deceased daughter. This cannot be true. I refuse to believe it. Stacy sealed the envelope back and placed it in her desk draw thinking what to do next, I'll wait till Carl comes home. Stacy went home that night in deep thought.

"Hey, Stacy, did you have a rough day. You seem a little distant."

"Not my best day, except for our time together at lunch."

"So, let's go back to that point and start, put everything else out of your mind. I made dinner. Let's eat and go for a walk or a movie."

"Let's survive dinner first, I thought you said you didn't cook."

"True, I don't usually cook, but I can burn a pot or two."

"Oh, Gosh, I only have two pots, did you destroy both of them."

As Margarite sucks her teeth, she said: "Sit down and eat."

They enjoyed a great meal and then set out for a movie. After staring at the marquee for several minutes, they left and stopped at a nearby comedy club for a few laughs and drinks. Stacy was able to place the Geremy story out of her head and wait for Carl.

Geremy's frustration continued to grow. Not knowing if she picked up the letter. Her behavior had not changed, nor did she ask any questions. Then the most puzzling of all if she didn't get it who did? He was driving his self-further insane.

Carl returned home on Friday evening the ladies picked him up at the airport. He asked how they were doing, and Margarite said, "My big sister here took care of everything, we're good."

"Great!" as he looked over to Stacy. He sensed that something was wrong, but he figured that she wanted to discuss it privately.

"So, what do we do tonight? I slept on the plane."

"Well we found this nice comedy club, and tonight they debut a new artist. You up to it, Stacy."

"Yes, let's do it."

The next morning Margarite went for a short run. While she was away, Carl asked Stacy what was on her mind.

"I did not tell you, when I first started with the firm Geremy approached me and we went to dinner, only dinner nothing further, but he began stalking me the next morning and that evening."

"What do you mean, stalking you?"

"He parked his car in the parking area and watched for when I would go out and come in. I did not want anything to do with him or any other male in the firm after that. Then I met you and things were coming along nicely. That first 3-day weekend that we went away is when I found out he was your friend. I did not want to lose you over something I should have confronted when it happened."

"You should have told me."

"I know that now and when Margarite told me her story I knew at that moment, he was doing the same thing and I had to go and confront him in person. Let him know I know how he operates and to leave Margarite alone."

"Well, thank you for protecting my sister, I plan on talking to him later today."

"Before you do that, take a look at this", Margarite hands Carl the envelope.

"What's this 'THE TRUTH.'"

"Geremy left this on my chair in my office."

"Is this true."

Stacy shrugs her shoulders.

"It can't be true, have you spoken to him about it."

"No, I'll leave that up to you."

"This is Crazy. Does Margarite know?"

"No"

Carl grabs his phone and sends a text to Geremy, let's meet today at 12 at the gym.

"This is Crazy"

Carl and Geremy met at their favorite Bar, meet at the gym is a code that they set up years ago for their favorite Bar. It's where their eyes got the most exercise.

"Hey Carl, welcome back, how was Hawaii?"

"It was a good trip. But that's not why we are here. Why are you messing with my sister?

"I wasn't messing with her. After the time we spent while she was carrying the baby, I enjoyed her company. I told her and she got scared and said that she looked at me as a second brother."

"Look, your story and her story isn't adding up. She is not interested in you, and I'm telling you to stay away from my sister."

"Alright"

"Now what's with this other bullshit, that the baby is yours."

"So, Stacy did get my letter."

"Hell, yes she got your letter. Why would you try to scare her like that? and is there any truth in it."

"Yes, the baby is mine."

"you know you're really fucked up in the head, I don't believe you. From the feelings that I received from Harry and Angelica's parents about how she lived her life and loved Harry, there is no way she would have cheated on him with you. Why are you making up these lies?"

"Great! You spoke with them about the letter."

"Hell No!!, This is Crazy. You need psychiatric help."

"We had sex during the time I was closing my mother's house."

"Really, this is not a dream, it truly happened. Tell me more detail about how it happened."

"Dude, I'm not going to discuss my sex life with you, although I will say it was the best sexual experience of my life."

"I don't want to know about the sex, how did it lead up to it."

"Like I said we were closing the house, it was late, and we both were getting tired. I mentioned instead of going back to her parents' house she stay here. She thought that would not be appropriate. I reminded her of the many times we stayed together growing up, and now that the house is closed, it feels creepy. So, she stayed, and we talked longer, she said she often wondered what if we had dated, would we still be together today or even married. We stopped talking and just stared into each other's eyes. She placed her hand on my face and said in all that time we never kissed. She pulled me closer, and it all started with a kiss."

"Wow! It sounds like a very emotional time, but why do you think the baby is yours. She was married."

"Well, she never told me about Harry and was not wearing a ring."

"yeah, but why do you think the baby is yours."

"After the train accident, is when I found out about their marriage and the fertility drugs that she was taking to produce more eggs to freeze. I'm sure that they were probably told to hold off on sex because there would be a greater risk of having a baby during this time, and since we did have sex, its simple mathematics."

"It sounds like it has some baring, but are you prepared to rip up their lives for this. I know that Harry has been the perfect father, and the Olswains are the best."

"How do you know this?'

"Harry and I never lost contact. Peter looks at me as an uncle."

"Stop, this is why we stopped our bar visits because you have been playing uncle to my child."

"Whoa, Whoa, hey control yourself. No one knew about this alleged affair."

"Alleged? You still do not believe me."

"I don't know what to think."

"Well, go ask your new best friend if they were having sex. This guy has taken everything from me, you, Angelica, the baby — my whole life."

Geremy gets up from the Bar and storms out. Carl is left completely confused. Does he bring this up with Harry and the Olswains, Is Geremy capable of doing something rash against Harry. Carl needed someone on the outside of all this to talk too, but who?

He rose from his bar seat, paid the bill and left. He wasn't in the mood to go back home and play 20 questions with Stacy. So, he drove around, trying to clear his thoughts. He finally decided that he needed to see Peter. He called Harry and told him that he picked up a few things for Peter while in Hawaii and wanted to drop them off. Harry was pleased to hear Carl's voice and told him to come on over. When he arrived at the house, he removed the presents from the trunk that he loaded earlier before leaving his house. As he approached the door, Harry opened it and yelled back to Peter,

"Peter, look who's here, Uncle Carl."

Carl entered to see Peter clumsily moving about in his walker. Of course, he is looking to see if there are any signs that he resembles Geremy.

"Hey, little man, look at what I brought back from Hawaii."

Carl sat and played with Peter, he enjoyed playing the Uncle role. As he started getting tired, Harry put him to sleep.

Harry asked about the trip, they talked and laughed. Harry never asked about Margarite before, but this time he did.

"How is your sister doing?"

"Margarite? She's doing excellent. Her modeling career has really taken off."

"I saw a fashion show on the television, and I thought that this one girl looked like Margarite. It was in Europe—Italy or Spain. I don't remember where."

"That was her"

"I assume she no longer does surrogate work."

"No, you were her one and only."

"Well, I think about her every night when I put Peter to bed. What a special gift she gave me."

They talked a little longer before Carl left. Carl new that Stacy needed some answers. It was time to go home.

Harry, however, was not completely honest with Carl. He thinks about Margarite all the time. He remembers her warm smiles when they would go for walks. The way she would read stories to a child that would not be hers. The way she proudly stood by Angelica's casket at the funeral. Margarite is a woman of grit and integrity. The type of woman that catches his attention.

When Carl walked into the house, Stacy let him know that Margarite returned to her apartment.

"What did he say."

"He tried to say that Margarite misunderstood his conversation. I told him, regardless stay away from my sister."

"and What about THE TRUTH"

"The story he laid down was pretty convincing. His story is that while they were closing his mother's house, she approached him and kissed him and everything else just followed."

"I'm shocked that they had an affair to the point of disbelief but still how does he know it's his kid and not Harry's."

"He said that when a woman takes fertility drugs to increase egg generation that they are told to sustain from sex to prevent having an egg fertilized."

"Knowing this makes the thought of an affair even more unbelievable. Why would Angelica take the chance of having unprotected sex during this time? I don't buy in on the heat of the moment philosophy. This woman was not ready to have children and the regiment of preparation required to freeze your eggs is mentally and physically challenging, only to throw it away on a one-night stand. That's Bullshit! I don't believe it. So, what do we do now?"

"I went to visit Harry and Peter."

"Why, were you going to tell him."

"I stopped by to see if Peter looked like Geremy."

"Carl, you didn't"

"I did, I mean I dropped off the presents I bought in Hawaii and looked to see if he looked like Geremy."

"Did he?"

"Not to me, he didn't."

"But something interesting did happen."

"What?"

"Harry asked about Margarite and mentioned that he saw her on TV at a Fashion show. He thinks about her every evening when he puts Peter to sleep. That's the first time he's asked about her?"

"Margarite will be happy to hear that."

"Why?"

"Sit down. Remember, when Margarite was caught in the fires."

"Yeah"

"Harry was the first responder that took her from the flames. She's been googly eyes over him ever since."

"So that's why she took the surrogate assignment so soon after signing up because it was him. How do you know this?"

"We are sisters now, and sisters talk."

"I'm glad you to are comfortable with each other. It's good to have a happy, caring family."

Chapter 13:
Peter's Coma

Meanwhile, for Geremy, there is no happiness. Now that he's let the cat out of the bag, he has no fears of moving forward. So, he prepares a similar letter of THE TRUTH to send to the Olswains. Carl decided to use Dave as his outside person to confide in. He told him what Geremy did to his sister and the letter he left for Stacy.

"Geremy left a letter for Stacy on her office chair making claims that the baby was his. I talked to him about that, and he claims that this poor dead girl came on to him when they were closing down his mother's house. In fact, let's see, how did he phrase it, oh yeah 'It was the best sexual experience he's had in his life'"

"Wait, say that last part again."

"Best sexual experience that he had in his life. What's clicking in your mind."

"Remember last year when Geremy was exploring dark sexual encounters with fetish groups."

"How can I forget."

"Stay with me here. It all started with that guy we met in the bar. Uhm what was his name…, Austin!"

"Yeah"

"You don't remember … Geremy said that Austin after fucking his dead wife it was the best sexual experience he had ever had. That's what set Geremy off, he was trying to find the same experience. He was with Angelica as she was dying right."

"You're saying that he …, No."

"it fits."

"No way."

"Hey, you know Geremy has to talk about his sexual pleasures. It's like his second high, and I doubt if he could keep something this big inside. So, if he didn't tell you or me who else could he have told."

"Austin?"

"Yeah Austin"

"We have to see if we can find him. What else do you remember from that night."

Carl and Dave struggled to recreate that evening and the many talks with Geremy after.

The Olswains received a special delivery letter package from Geremy. Peter was out, and only Macie was home. When Peter arrived back at the house, he found Macie curled up in the box window seat in the kitchen, crying.

"Macie! What's wrong baby?"

She turns to him, clutching the letter in her hands. As Peter pulls the letter from her hands, she says, "How do we tell Harry."

"Tell Harry, what? ". As Peter begins to read the letter, his concerned expression moves to complete rage.

"This is pure garbage. I know my daughter and cheating on Harry is not in her character. I may not have known Harry long, but for the time I have, it's evident that he loved Angelica. That type of love can only be achieved by having your partner love you the same. This bastard was too afraid even to ask my daughter out as a child now he's going to try and scandalize her name in death. I'm going to the city."

"To do what?"

"TO FIND THE TRUTH!"

"Maybe we should take a moment, Sleep on it, get your anger in check before we head off."

"There you go trying to put a plan together and not react at the moment. Well, not this time, Macie, are you coming with me."

"No, you're not thinking straight, and I know as you proceed on the road, you will realize that and come back. I'll be right here."

Peter leaves the house and drives off in the car. The words of the letter and Macie's words were ringing loudly in his head. He was fully engulfed with rage towards Geremy, Peter feels a sharp pain. As he grabs his chest the car veered across the roadway and crashes into the fencing to a stop. Engine still running, other motorists stop and run to his aide. An ambulance is called, and they take him to the hospital. Macie is notified, and she rushes over. Macie walks into the hospital ER and screams;

"My name is Macie Olswain, my husband Peter was in a car accident and brought here."

The charge nurse rushes over and sits her down.

"Is he alright?"

"I will have to check with the doctor, would you care for some water?"

"I want to see my husband."

"Of Course. I will go see where he is. In the meantime, perhaps you could fill out these forms for me."

Macie pushes the forms away, "Please, my husband."

The charge nurse gets up and looks on the charts for Mr. Olswain. He had been taken from the ER to Surgery.

"Mrs. Olswain, your husband, was taken to Surgery."

"Surgery, oh my GOD, what happened."

"Come with me to a better place to discuss this."

The ER charge nurse takes Macie to the Surgical waiting area.

"Mrs. Olswain, this is the Surgical Triage nurse, she can better explain your husband's situation."

"Hello, would you care for some water."

"No"

"your husband has suffered a high-stress condition that damaged an artery to his heart. We had to perform immediate open-heart surgery to repair the artery."

Macie starts to cry, blaming herself. I always have to plan. If I had been in the car, I could have talked the rage down to a reasonable level. The nurse brings her a tissue from the nurses' desk.

"I cannot give you an update on his condition at the moment, but the doctor will come to see you and let you know."

"If perhaps you can help complete his admission forms: Does your husband have a highly stressful job, has he been under a lot of stress at home or has he had the flu lately."

"Peter was never sick, an occasional cold, but nothing major, Please, help him, I can't lose him. "

As Macie sat waiting for the surgery to end and the doctor to come and give her the news, she received a call from Harry.

"Hello, Macie, how are you?"

She responded, "I'm well," Macie did not want to tell Harry about Peter because she did not wish to inform him about the letter.

"Macie, What's wrong? I know something is wrong because you never respond to how are you without asking about little Peter. You sound sad, has something happened."

Macie breaks into tears again and says, "Peter is in the hospital, it's his heart." "What hospital are you at? I'll take Peter over to Carl and Stacy and be on my way.

Macie remembered that Carl was best friends with Geremy.

"No, don't leave Peter with them. Bring him with you, seeing him will do me good."

"I really don't want to bring him into a hospital. He'll be fine with them."

"NO! I HAVE MY REASONS"

"Macie, calm down. I know you're worried about Peter, but I'm little Peter's father."

"You don't understand, Geremy put Peter into the hospital."

At that moment, the doctor approached Macie.

"Are you Mrs. Olswain."

"Yes, I am"

Macie hangs up the phone, so she can speak with the doctor. Harry could hear the doctor asking questions before the phone cut-out. Now he's wondering what's going on. Was Geremy at the house and he drove Peter to the hospital. Is that what she meant by 'Geremy put Peter into the hospital".

Harry placed a call to Carl on his cell phone.

"Hello, Harry, perfect timing. I just came out of a meeting, what's up."

"I was just speaking with Macie, she's at the hospital, something about Peter's heart."

"Little Peter?"

"No, her husband."

"You want us to stay with little Peter while you go to the hospital?

"Yes, but Macie said not to leave Peter with you. It's something to do with Geremy. She wasn't making a lot of sense. I have to get there, but I do not want to take Peter into a frantic hospital scene."

"No worries, I'm coming over."

Carl walked over to Stacy's office to see how the rest of her day looked. Her calendar was filled with meetings. He informed his admin of his emergency and to reschedule the rest of his day. Carl went alone to Harry's house.

Geremy walked into Stacy's office after Carl left and asked: "I could not help overhearing, is there something wrong with my baby."

Stacy turned her back to him instructed Geremy to get the Hell out of her office.

Geremy was persistent and did not move, "I have a right to know."

As she turned to fully unleash her fury upon him she noticed the members of a scheduled meeting starting to enter the room, Geremy backed up to the doorway. Stacy asked the last member to shut the door. During the meeting, she saw Geremy pacing back and forth in the hall and finally move quickly towards the exit.

Carl arrives at Harry's house they talk very briefly reiterating Macie's conversation then Harry leaves for the hospital.

At the hospital, "Mrs. Olswain, your husband, suffered a thoracic aneurysm, a break in the blood vessel traveling from his heart. We were able to catch it in time and repair it. So, he is out of risk for any heart failure. Unfortunately, he has gone into a coma. This is very rare but sometimes happens to patients that undergo this type of surgery. I have seen recoveries in days, weeks, and years. At this time, it's a wait and see.

He is being prepared to be taken to a room, someone will come and get you. "

Harry made it to the hospital while Macie was still in the Surgical waiting room.

"Macie, I'm here, how is he?

They embraced, and she told Harry what the doctor said.

"You've been here for a while, I know you're not thinking about yourself at the moment, but we do need to get you something to eat. Let me see if the nurses can tell us how long before Peter will be assigned a room."

Harry approached the nursing desk, "Excuse me, can you tell me how long before Mr. Olswain will be given a room."

"Well, he's in the recovery unit now so it will probably be at least another hour or two."

"Thank you."

"Macie it will be another hour or 2 before we can see him. Don't worry, we won't leave the hospital, let's go to the cafeteria, OK?"

"I guess I am a little hungry."

"Great"

They walked to the cafeteria. Macie's mind was so centered on her husband that she did not notice that Harry was there alone. As they looked over the cafeteria menu, there was a kid's meal. Although Peter is not old enough to eat from the kid's meal, it triggered the thought of Peter in her mind.

"Harry, where is little Peter?"

"Carl is watching him at my house."

"No…"

"Macie, let's get our food, sit down, and you tell me what's going on."

They collected their food and drinks and sat down.

"Let's eat a little food first, then we will talk."

While they were eating Carl gets a call from Stacy. "Honey, have you heard from Harry?"

"No, I haven't."

"What if he doesn't come home tonight? Have you fed Peter?

"Harry fed him before I got here. "

"Do you need me to come over?"

"No, Babe, one of us should get some sleep."

"Here's something you should know, Geremy walked into my office after you left. He said that he overheard your conversation and wanted to know if his baby was sick."

"What did you say?"

"I told him to get the Hell out of my office, and a few minutes later, I saw him rushing to the exit. Does he know where Harry lives?

"No"

"Call Margarite and the two of you stay together tonight."

"Call me back when you're together."

Harry and Macie were halfway through their meal when Macie received a text. She was still fixed on Peters' welfare and did not hear the repeated ring tones. Harry brought it to her attention. She removed the phone from her bag and placed it next to her on the table. When the ringtones played again the name of the sender appeared on the screen, her hands balled into a clenched fist, she slid her chair back in fear and anger. The name of the sender was Geremy. Harry grabbed the phone. Macie looked at Harry shaking her head from side to side in a manner to mean 'don't answer it' but not a word came from her mouth. The message was sent 10 times, 'Where is my baby?'

"Macie, do you know what this means?"

Macie again could not speak, and another text came through with the same words.

Harry did not return a text he called the number.

"It's about time, where is my child? I have a right to know."

"what are you talking about."

Geremy was stunned for a second to hear Harry's voice.

"Geremy, I know this is you. What are you talking about?"

"You have my child?"

"Are you crazy, what child and why are you harassing Macie."

" The baby at your house is mine."

"Are you talking about Peter."

"So, that's my son's name?"

"No, that's my son's name. Why would you think that my son is yours and why are you harassing Macie with this nonsense?"

"Because your wife made love to me before she died. That's right she cheated on you with the man she truly loved. It hurts to find out the truth, doesn't it? Now you feel the pain I felt when you bolted into the train and pushed me back away from her. Then telling me that she was your wife as you swept her away in a different ambulance. You bastard, how do you feel now?"

"This is crazy, and you're crazy. Angelica and I spoke every evening into the morning while she was away. Including the night, she stayed at your place. She was feeling uneasy with you. In fact, that morning, Angelica could hear you pacing back and forth outside her locked door. She placed me on hold and called Macie to come pick her up.

Macie, don't you remember this?"

Macie breaks her silence, "Yes, Yes, I do." Her hands became unclenched. The stress in her face lightened.

"So, I don't know where your deranged mind has taken you, but my Angelica did not touch you, but I will. Keep looking behind you, in front of you and around you, cause one day I will be there."

Harry hangs up the phone, "What does this have to do with Peter being in this hospital?"

Macie told him about the letter, Peter's rage against Geremy, the accident and the surgery. Now Harry was consumed with the same anger, but the fear that this idiot may try to abduct little Peter was greater. He picked up his phone and called Carl.

Carl answers "Harry, how is Peter?"

"We don't know yet. I just finished talking to your friend Geremy.

"Geremy is no longer my friend. "

"Did you know that he thinks Peter is his?"

"He gave Stacy a letter that day I stopped by to see you and Peter after my trip. I was going to tell you, but his story was so compelling I did not know if it was true or not. What does this have to do with Peter in the hospital, and how did he get your number?"

"I need you to bring Peter to me now. On my way."

Carl hangs up the phone and calls Stacy, "Carl, what's the news."

"Do you have Margarite?"

"Yes, she's here."

"Good, both of you get in the car and come to the hospital have your Taser with you. Geremy sent the

Olswain's a Truth letter and Peter had a heart attack after reading it. Harry spoke to Geremy, and now he wants me to bring little Peter to the hospital ASAP. Meet me there and keep an eye out for Geremy."

Macie and Harry finished eating and went back to the waiting area. The nurse informed them that Peter had been moved to a room and they could visit with him. They did not know what to expect upon entering the room. Rumbling through their minds were thoughts of open-heart surgery, and in a coma, they expected to see the worst; several I-V's, life support machines…. As the door opened, they heard Peters voice fussing with the nurse trying to give him something to drink. He looked to the door and with great delight, said, "Macie, you're here."

Macie took to crying plentiful tears of joy.

"You old goat, I should have known that you could not stay in a coma."

They embraced and kissed.

"I'm not ready to leave you yet. The doctor said I probably had this aneurism hiding here for years. "

"I was so scared. I should have been with you."

"You did the right thing. Otherwise, we both may be sitting in this hospital."

Peter looked towards the door and saw Harry, "Harry, where's little Peter?"

"On his way."

Macie tells Peter, "Harry knows."

"He knows what?"

"I know about the letter, and I also know that Angelica stayed true to me. Just relax and get stronger, I'll take care of Geremy."

Carl and little Peter arrived at the hospital first. He calls Harry from the car.

"Hi Carl, are you here."

"Yes, what do you want me to do."

"I'll be right down."

Stacy and Margarite drive up before Harry gets there. They get out of the car and Margarite runs to Carl.

"Are you alright? why are we at the hospital?"

As she looks down at the car, "Who's baby is that?"

Just then, Harry comes outside. "Margarite?"

"Harry?"... "What's going on?"

Carl looks at Harry, "I could not leave them there with Geremy running around."

"I understand, Margarite it's good to see you."

"You too."

Geremy was stalking Stacy, he had parked in the parking area by her house. He followed her to pick up Margarite and then to the hospital.

Harry reached into the car to pull out Peter. Margarite places both hands over her heart, "He is so beautiful."

Geremy yelled to them as he got out of his car in the parking lot, "That's my child."

Just at that moment, the parking lot exploded with police lights. Geremy was stopped before reaching them and taken into custody as a person of interest.

Totally confused on what just happened Harry, little Peter, Carl, Stacy, and Margarite turned and entered the hospital.

Harry looks at Carl, "Did you call the police."

"No, I thought you did."

"Stacy did you."

"I'm as shocked as you guys."

Stacy changes the subject, "Harry is Peter still in a coma."

Confused Margarite yells out, "a coma, what is going on here"

"Oh yeah, I have good news, Peter is out of the coma and is sitting up talking. I'm sure he will be happy to see all of you."

They open the door to heart filled smiles. Harry and little Peter enter first, "there's my namesake." Followed by Carl and Stacy, Macie grabs Carl's hand, "Thank you for watching over him." and before the door can close, in walks Margarite. Macie embraces her and says, "My child, I have missed you and think about you often."

Conversations broke out like a family would typically have. Making plans for when Peter gets out. No more separations. No one was ready to talk about the elephant in the room—What to do about Geremy? Where was he taken? Who made a call to the police?

They stayed with Peter until the nurse through them out. Carl, Stacy, and Margarite left first. Followed by Harry and little Peter. Macie stayed with Peter in his room, the nurses rolled in another bed.

Chapter 14:
Dave's Identity

Carl received a call from Dave while in route to the hospital. "Hi Dave, I can't talk to you now. I'm taking little Peter to the hospital."

"Is he sick?"

"No, his grandfather is in the hospital, something about Geremy being the reason why he's there, I don't know?"

"Ok, I'll let you go, we'll talk later."

Dave was fixed on finding Austin. He searched for his name in the state of Michigan with no match's against Austin's description. So, he began searching for necrophilia related crimes. Dave was appalled by the number of these types of occurrences happening nationwide, then he found an article about a couple in New Mexico. The headline read Kayak couple death rape. The article told about a couple that met on a dating site and decided to meet in person on a Kayaking adventure. The victim had told a friend where they were going and to give a call in 3 hours to check in. When she had not heard from her friend in 4 hours, she reached out to another friend in the National Park Patrol. Two park patrol officers set out to the area of the park designated for kayaking, upon their arrival, they found the two of them committing a sexual act on the rocks. They commanded them to cease and to put on their clothes. The man did not stop, and the woman looked lifeless. The two officers moved in and pulled the naked man off of her. They saw that her wetsuit had been pulled down to her knees, her head bleeding. There was a rock with blood on it just above her head. Austin was arrested for the crime and sent to a mental institution to await trial, where he escaped.

Dave then searched the hospital records and found that 2-1/2 years ago, the electrical system at the hospital had a significant power glitch losing all power for 1 hour. There were 3 inmates in the yard at the time, two were quickly captured, but 1 escaped, it was Austin. So where is he now and how did he get to Sacramento. Dave continued his search, and suddenly he noticed a pattern of these occurrences from New Mexico to

Sacramento. Austin was a serial killer. Dave knew what to do with this information and contacted the US Marshal services. He asked if they still had a manhunt out for Austin, who escaped from the NMBHI two-plus years ago. Three plain-clothed US Marshalls visited Dave the next day to look over the data and to find out why Dave had an interest.

Dave explained to them the scene at a bar 1 year ago where he met Austin and the strange behavior of Geremy from that meeting to now. The Marshalls also made Dave aware of a local homicide involving a woman's body found in a field, strangled. Her assaulter also committed necrophilia. The time of her death runs in the same timeline of when Dave said he met Austin. The local police went back to the area hotel bars and circulated Austin and Geremy's pictures, not expecting to get a hit after a year, but they did, a bartender and one of the servers at the hotel remembered both of them. Apparently, the deceased woman travels into town quite often, and her usual habit is to pick up someone at the bar, leave with him and return the next day. It happened so often that the bartender and server would place wagers on whom she would pick up. This time was different, there were two men. The one doing most of the talking, she gave her number too. Then he whispered in her ear, and they left. She did not leave with them instead she left the bar and went to the elevator for the rooms. When asked if she had returned to the hotel lately, they both replied that they had not seen her since then.

The Marshall unit in search of Austin moved to Sacramento and took office. A warrant was put out for Geremy, as a person of interest in the local homicide. Based on Carl's conversation with Dave, the Marshals set up a perimeter around the hospital. Dave's name and any reference that he had contacted the US Marshall was kept out of the reports. Dave used to be a State Trooper in Kansas, and his wife was a US Marshall. She was part of an undercover sting operation that went sour, and she shot and killed the son of a prominent criminal. The US Marshalls placed her and her family into the protective custody program.

Chapter 15:
Where is Austin?

The next day was business as usual, with the absence of Geremy. The police and US Marshall questioned Geremy about Austin. When was your last contact? Do you have a way of contacting him? When was the last time you saw the lady at the hotel bar?

Geremy was placed in a line-up and picked out by the bartender and the bar server. They searched his phone and found a text dated one day after being rescued from the train accident to an unknown number in his database. The message read, 'I now know the feeling of ultimate sexual pleasure, you were right. My first true love on a train — fantastic'.

The Marshalls were able to track down the whereabouts of Austin from the telephone number used to receive and send text messages. They told Austin that he almost got away because the other guy that they arrested was starting to chalk up more kills.

"What are you talking about, who has more kills?"

"Geremy"

"Geremy? What that putz from Sacramento. Hell, he doesn't even know how to pick up a woman in a bar or any other place. He's got his friends fooled thinking that he spends his weekends performing one-night stands. Until he met me, the only thing he performed nightly was pumping his own cock. He's only got one kill, some bitch on a train. I don't even think he killed her. The earthquake probably killed her, but he did fuck her while she was dead. He did tell me that. So, what other kills is he talking about?

The Marshalls wanted to help Dave and get this creep off the street, but the evidence against Geremy was too weak to pass onto the District Attorney's office. It would be considered informational evidence at best; all they had was a text message from Geremy to Austin, which became the key evidence leading to the recapture of a wanted felon, the testimony from a psychotic convict that Geremy said he committed an act of necrophilia. Two letters written by Geremy proclaiming he had sexual consent from Angelica.

The body of evidence is buried. No autopsy was performed, the cause of death was attributed to the earthquake and the train derailment. The family did not wish to disturb Angelica's eternal rest by exhuming her body.

Dave's wife was starting to get a little nervous at this point. "Dave, you were a great trooper, and I know your whole life was centered around putting the bad guys away, but Honey, you have to let this case go. You've done all you can, let the Marshals take it over. What if your name or picture leaks out or if you are called to testify on what happened that night at the bar, then you, me, our children are all dead or forced to be re-routed to some new place, with new names, new identities. Is that what you want? Honey, please let it go."

The endangerment of his family and the life they put together here forced Dave to back off. He made sure that his involvement was eradicated entirely from the files. It was replaced with an unknown informant.

Geremy was released and thanked publicly for his aid in capturing Austin – a hero.

Geremy wasn't finished, his anger deepened with the knowledge that they are all acting like a family and the nerve of them collectively filing a protective order against him. Geremy was now a hero and with his newly found fame and public support, he elected to use it to submit a charge of child abduction against the family through the legal system.

Chapter 16:
The Trials

Geremy's new hero status aided him in obtaining an audience with the top law firm in Sacramento. He told his version of the story, and that his purpose for securing their services was to get his child back. His story raised a few eyebrows, had there ever been a case before the courts questioning the legitimacy of the implanted zygote into a surrogate mother. This could be a first, and with Geremy's instant public recognition to take on the case would elevate the firms' name also. The Firm told Geremy that it is a case with merit, we need to deliberate and draft up a contract for him to sign. They made plans to reconvene at 3 pm the next day. Geremy walked out neglecting to inform the Firm about the letters he wrote, or the call records collected from Harry's phone.

The next day the Firm presented Geremy with contractual documents to allow him to solicit their services. Geremy eagerly signed the contract and shook hands.

"Great, what's our first step."

"Well, first, we will need proof of legitimacy."

"How?"

"We will petition the court for a DNA sample from the child if the test comes back true to match yours, 'Wah Lahr!', Legitimacy. So, you will be receiving a letter from the clinic to come down for a DNA test, it's just a swab of your mouth. Please refrain from all attempted contact with any of the named parties.

Now, Let's go and win your baby."

"Thank you."

It took about a week to get a court order for a DNA sample. A member of the Sheriff's department and a court-appointed nurse arrived at Harry's door. The order handed to Harry had Geremy's name in it. Harry was reluctant, what if Geremy was right, I can't lose Peter. At that moment Angelica's picture fell from the table. All doubt was erased from Harry's mind, and he went to get Peter. The nurse was very kind and gentle, Peter seemed to like her. She took a sample from Peter and Harry. In the paperwork it indicated a date for the two parties to meet in court to hear the results, it also detailed what Harry would need to do to get a copy of the report. The court date was set for 2 weeks. Harry called the family to inform them of what happened and what was to come.

The entire family arrived at the courtroom for the paternity reading. Geremy was there with his team of lawyers, waiting for the results to be announced to file claims for the abduction of a minor.

You could see the expectancy in their faces, like a cat watching a mouse it's about to eat.

The judge entered the room, everyone took their seats. He spoke of the tragedy that placed these men in their present position. One is bearing the sorrow of losing his wife in an earthquake. The other having to shoulder the sin of adultery, not knowing that his childhood love was married at the time. Both men grieving her loss and wanting to raise the child. Paternity cases where the child is fixed in a loving family never have a satisfactory ending. He then asked for both men to stand, and he read the DNA results. "the rightful father of Peter by the DNA results is

Harry Albert." The family jumped up from their seat and yelled for joy.

Geremy in full dismay lost himself and shouted out in the courtroom. "That's a lie, I was the last man to make love to her — no one else was on that train. What we shared as she laid dying was more sensational that I could ever have expected. That child is mine. This isn't over, this will never be over until that baby is with his rightful father, Me."

The bailiff held Harry back from going after Geremy. The courtroom was cleared. The Firm representing Geremy approached Harry and offered their card.

"We are sorry for putting you and the family through this ordeal. If you would like for us to represent you in a case against Geremy, we will be honored, and it would be Pro-Bono."

In the few days following the decision, Carl explained to Harry that he was sorry for having doubts about little Peter's origin. Geremy's story that a couple undergoing this type of procedure are told to forego any sexual activity was too plausible to disregard. Harry admitted that they were asked to refrain from sex. A couple of nights before Geremy's mothers funeral Angelica informed Harry that Geremy was the love of her life that never flourished. Harry asked Angelica if he should be worried about her seeing her old heartthrob, she said No, and they made love that night.

Harry accepted the Firms offer and brought charges against Geremy. The Firm had the arduous task to convince a jury on two resolutions; The first, Rape, the jurors had to believe that necrophilia was an act of an unwanted and un-consensual sex act. The second, murder, the cause of Angelica's death was due to the stopping of lifesaving actions to fulfill a sexual fantasy.

In the weeks and months to follow, the Firm collected evidence: Statements of multiple stalking incidents, Statements from fellow co-workers describing Geremy's obsession for necrophilia, Comments from fetish members of his exploration into sexual fetish acts, his "The Truth" letters, the testimony of the convicted serial killer, phone records and his recorded outburst during the paternity courtroom hearing.

Geremy's court-appointed lawyer explained to him that "The Firm" would probably be able to prove rape. Although their evidence he felt was weak, it would probably be enough to sway the sentiment of the jury. How they could take the same evidence and prove murder he felt was impossible. Angelica was thrown from her seat on the train 30 feet against the front of the train car. That's the cause of death. He asked Geremy to plead guilty for the rape and let's try to get the murder conviction thrown out. Geremy refused.

The Firm knew that they needed to attack Geremy's character first, after all, he was seen as a hero for helping to capture Austin. The Firm used the testimony of Stacy and Margarite, coupled with his capture at the hospital as proof of stalking. Then they introduced the recorded outburst during the paternity courtroom hearing to legitimize the Rape Accusation.

Proving the case for murder was the challenge, they needed to determine intent and convince the jury that the cause of death was not brought on by the earthquake. The Firm presented the evidence in the best manner that they could, however, the accusation of murder was in doubt even into the closing arguments. Geremy's attorney was first to present the closing arguments. In which he stated," after the train came to a halt Geremy rushed to Angelica, moving rubble from around her body, he felt a light pulse and started administering CPR. It wasn't until after several attempts to revive her that he stopped. Knowing that his efforts were not going to make a difference."

Now it was the Firms turn, as the lead attorney approached the jurors the words from Geremy's attorney rang loudly in her mind. She wrote a new closing argument as she spoke, she argued that based on the closing statement by the defense, Angelica was alive after the accident. She cited that Geremy was not a doctor, he had CPR knowledge and training. Training that prepared you to know that as long as there was a pulse, however light, he should have continued performing CPR, yet by his own actions he stopped. The entire defense was based on one fact. The fact that Geremy could not have accomplished these outlandish attacks against Angelica, because she was the love of his life.

Well, love gives you extra strength to endure in times of disaster and stress, like the timid woman who lifted a vehicle off her child, allowing him to be pulled to safety.

Where was Geremy's extra strength, his backup drive to keep Angelica alive?

It was switched to a new goal, his obsession with the notion of necrophilia, the idea of experiencing the best sexual pleasure possible, as told to him by a psychotic serial killer. Saving Angelica was no longer the higher calling, achieving his fetish desire became the prize and he stopped all rescue efforts and raped her. It was this single act of eroticism that brought about the death of Angelica.

Now as you go back and deliberate this case. I want you to place yourself in the body of Angelica, lying on the floor of that train unable to move, unable to speak and feeling your life fading but not giving up, grasping at every hope for life because the man you know, the man you can trust is working hard to breathe life back into you.

You are Angelica and you are not dead. This man that has been with you for your entire life is now going to save you, but before you call him a hero, I want you to feel what comes next. This man who claims he loves you stops CPR, undresses you, removes your undergarments and plunges his penis into you, again and again, until he releases his pint up passion inside of you. The horror of the event causes you to lose all hope and desire to survive.

Then I want you to leave Angelica's body and as a jury come back in this courtroom with a conviction of Rape and Murder. —Thank you.

The jury made up of men and women deliberated for 12 hours and returned a unanimous verdict of guilty to Rape and Murder.

The Olswains, Stacy, Margarite, and Harry were pleased that it was over. For Carl and Dave, their scars run a little deeper, they unselfishly take some of the blame of what changed their friend and co-worker. Had they not left him with this stranger his mind would not have been twisted. Maybe he could have saved Angelica. The what if's of that night will always be a part of them.

During sentencing, the judge stated that due to the extraordinary circumstances of this case, Geremy would serve two life sentences for the Rape and the Murder of Angelica. This is the first time a rape conviction ever received a life sentencing. His sentence was to start at a psychiatric prison hospital for 3 years or until he was determined to be mentally stable to be placed into the general population at the state penitentiary.

Chapter 17:
The New Austin

Due to the nature of Geremy's offenses, his trial was televised on the major networks – entitled from Hero to Madman. As you recall Geremy was deemed a hero for his assistance in apprehending Austin.

It was going on Geremy's 6th month in the psychiatric ward when he received a letter. Geremy did not recognize the sender of the letter but did notice that for most of the inmates, their letters were opened before they received them, this letter was not. He opened the letter and he realized that it was from Austin.

Austin knew his way around the prison system and the public airing of his involvement in Geremy's case brought him a favorable fan base, some of which were in the prison system both behind bars and not.

Austin started the letter taunting Geremy with the facts of Angelica's death, brought out during the trial, especially the point made by the attorney that Angelica was not dead at the time of the sexual assault. Austin wrote you muddled your only chance to feel ultimate domination and enjoyment over the woman that brought him his most in-depth source of pain. He stated to Geremy that he had not completed his task to achieve the pleasure that they had discussed. Austin took on the tone of the teacher to the student, the first time is always the hardest. This time you had an Angel on your side that assisted you with an earthquake, you simply needed to finish by placing your hand over her nose and mouth to stop her from breathing, then mount her and feel the joy, but don't give up, never give up, your time will still come.

Austin was very aware of the behavioral correctional drug program that Geremy was undergoing. He directed Geremy to keep this letter in a safe place and to read it every night.

He reminded Geremy of all the events that led up to where he was today. He wrote about their first meeting, that evening they remained at the club bar for a bit longer and instead of moving in on the ladies, Geremy fell into a drunken fit of self-pity over his personal love life. How his hidden love for Angelica had made him isolated to the pleasures of another woman. Austin took pleasure in Geremy's babble and feeling the vulnerability of the moment decided to take on the task of freeing him from her. He dragged Geremy from the club bar scene to scout hotel bars. He explained the women there are more relaxed, from out-of-town and have a room. While they searched, they drank, and while they drank, Austin convinced Geremy that Angelica was like all women, not willing to be pleased by the good man before them instead they look past him into the crowd for that guy with an edge - The man that can show her love but not be in love. Only having to come back to the good man and bleed out their hurt in tears, asking, Why does this happen over and over. A story no man really wants to hear, but for the good man, if this is the only way that he can feel close to her, he takes it and listens, advises, cleans her up and puts her to bed. Leaving with no satisfaction of his own, kicking himself for being such a patsy and a fool. Stuck in the same pattern repeating it over and over.

Austin continued to force this story into Geremy's drunken head throughout the night. Tonight, you're going to stand on your own two feet, tonight is the beginning of tomorrow. They arrived at the third hotel bar, walking in Austin shared eye contact with a woman sitting on a barstool, he sat Geremy at the end of the bar and told him to watch. Austin walked up to the woman and started a conversation, he mentioned that he felt her staring at him as they walked in the door. She admitted that she found him attractive. He found out that not only was she from out of town but that she was also from another state and would be at this hotel for 2 more nights. This was the detail he wanted to hear. He admitted he had an immediate attraction to her as well. But before they could explore the night together, he needed to get his friend home. She thought it very caring that he would not just abandon his friend. She asked for his phone and placed her number in it. She had some business emails to take care of and told him to go take care of his friend, call me on your way back to me. Austin dragged Geremy back to the club where they met and then told him the story of his wife on a kayaking trip and that he was going to achieve the same joy with the lady at the hotel.

The next day they spoke again Austin told Geremy that he was meeting her again for an early dinner, she was flying out on a 7:35 flight in the morning. He said to Geremy let's get together tomorrow night. Austin met with her that night for dinner, the conversation turned sexual, and they discussed different places they had sex or fantasized having sex. Austin explained how he would like to do it at night in the shadow area of a very public site, where they had to be very quiet to avoid detection - No matter how good the sex was feeling. She was very intrigued by this suggestion, especially after the exceptional and loud night they had in the hotel. She asked if he knew of a place that would fit the fantasy.

Just a block or two down from the hotel is a club, across the street is a building with tall columns in front. At night the streetlights cause the columns to cast a shadow against each other however there are times when the headlights of a turning car can cast light across the entire area. She placed her hand on Austin's knee; let's do it tonight, I'm wearing the perfect dress for it. She was wearing a sleeveless black open back dress with a very low-cut panel front. She instructed him to pay the bill while she went to the ladies room, there she reapplied her make-up and removed her panties.

As they approached the building, it was just as Austin described it. They quickly slid into the shadows, and Austin disrobed completely folding his clothes neatly and placing them on the ground. He took his socks and tied them together making a large knot, placing the knot into her mouth and tying the ends of the socks around her head. Austin smiled and told her that last night's vocal performance is still fresh in his mind. He placed his cheek on hers and slightly tug on her earlobe with his mouth and teeth, slowly moving his hands about her body he pulled up her dress around her ass, grabbing her butt cheeks firmly, pulling her against him. He untied the dress from her neck allowing for the top of her dress to droop revealing her breasts which he gently massaged with his hands, kissing her nipples and holding them firmly between his lips as he pulled away. He then moved down her body with his mouth and tongue, his hands pulled the dress down and it dropped to the ground releasing her naked body. Austin dropped to his knees with his mouth and tongue following the natural lines of her body, he reached his goal and used his tongue to excite her through masturbation. Her moans were starting to be heard through the socks, her breathing became heavier and her body was limbering that's when he stood straight up, grabbing and squeezing his hands tightly around her neck. As her last breath was leaving her body, he laid her down in the shadows of the pavement and completed his fantasy, sexually penetrating her with his cock again and again until he - until she was filled with his delight.

Austin had canvassed the area beforehand and knew that there was a field behind the building easily accessible from the side. He lifted her body and laid it in the field, returning to the front of the building and redressing.

He then walked across the street to the club and had a few drinks, engaging in conversation with several women.

The next night he met with Geremy with one intention, to introduce him to the dark side of sex. Austin told Geremy that he uses different fetishes to feed his fantasies and sexual hunger. He asked Geremy if he was ready to stand on his own two feet. Was he at a point to have Angelica removed from his thoughts freeing him to feel the pleasure of another woman? You saw that woman at the hotel bar, I had her for two nights. Come on in, let me show you what you have been missing. Austin introduced Geremy to a Dominatrix and told her the Angelica story.

The Dominatrix was an attractive woman, her leather outfit admittedly revealed her hour-glass figure, and the areas of visible skin were free of tattoos and piercings. She brought Geremy to the center of the room and asked him to remove his shirt. Geremy asked, Why? She showed her anger in his questioning and informed him that that was the last time he would speak to her, I tell you and you do it and when I want to hear your voice I will tell you to speak. Now place your hands in the cuffs of the chains hanging above you. She put a mask over his head and asked that he think only of Angelica. She grabbed a whip from the wall and began running the heal of the whip on his inner thighs. She told him that this is Angelica's hands touching you, she continued moving the whip up to his scrotum. This is Angelica teasing you and asked him if he wanted Angelica.

Geremy remained silent and she commanded him to answer. Geremy muttered with a low Yes. She laughed at him and replied the joy you crave from Angelica is denied leaving you with pain. As she was saying the words Angelica and Pain her whip sliced through the air against Geremy's back. He cried out in shock and in pain. She continued to taunt him, my name is Angelica, as she delivers another blow with the utterance of the name Angelica. This is how Angelica's love feels and the breaking of your heart, and another blow is delivered. She continued mocking his perceived love for Angelica whipping him on keywords; Angelica, Heart, Love and Pain. On words like Sex, Freedom, and Women, she would gently stroke his cock in an effort to arouse him. This continued for hours, and with each strike Geremy wanted it to end, but there were no safety words only the voice of the Dommes. I am Angelica, and this is the pain of my Love."

Austin brought Geremy back to her for an entire week. Telling Geremy this is how we release you from your childhood woes, Angelica was the dream of a child, and now as a man you know the pain she brings, this is the beginning of tomorrow. Remember.

At this point, the letter ended with the words Read This Every Evening, I will be back soon.

Geremy did as directed; Meds at 8am... Breakfast at 9am... Group Therapy at 10am... Lunch at Noon... Fresh air outside at 1pm... Psych session at 2:30pm... Game room at 3:30pm... Meds at 5pm... Dinner at 6pm... Lockdown at 8pm. After lockdown, he would read the letter. Repeating this pattern everyday... Repeat... Repeat... Repeat.

All of the work that the Group Therapy and Psych sessions were establishing each day, were washed away with the reading this well-constructed letter every evening. In fact, coupled with the drugs, the contents of the letter were ingrained so profoundly into Geremy's subconscious that it changed him. In his sessions, he began to show more resistance to their questions and his anger would peak on specific keywords.

It's been 4 weeks, and another unopened letter was brought to Geremy. It had a different name than before but still unknown to Geremy. In this letter, Austin praised Geremy for the control he was starting to show, as if he was there in the room. The control and power he should have had on the train to take him to the ultimate pleasure. The letter structure then changed like in the first letter driving his thoughts back to the fetish locations.

Remember the things we indulged ourselves in every night, not just the sessions with the Dommes, the multiple fetish rooms. How you were finally able to break from the Angelica spell and sexually express yourself with women and men alike. How you explored the freedom of No inhibitions. Sex with women of every ethnicity, weight, and height; sex with one and multiple women at a time. The realization of sexual pleasure through Orgies, Suffocation, Bondage, Master/Slave and Rape. Oh, how you expressed your joy and satisfaction in releasing your passion in another person's body after each session, now that your mind was free of Angelica. You spoke boldly of how Angelica no longer controlled you.

But we know that was not the case once you were with her again. The child in you longed for something you lost and filled your mind with a notion that she could still be yours. Your sort to abandon your teachings to rid yourself of Angelica but your lust for sexual satisfaction was to strong to deny. So you let your mind and body drift back to one of the fetishes that you enjoyed, which one was it Master/Slave; Bondage (since she could not move from her injuries) or was it Rape. I hope it was rape then you would have at least shown some aggressiveness towards her.

The letter continued going into exact detail on how and what acts were performed in the fetish rooms. Describing who and what area of the body the actions were affecting. It took Geremy back to how after each session, he would return to the Dommes and put on his mask and cuff himself back to the chains. How she would ask him to describe the experience was and say who he had fucked. If he could not remember the person's name or if he spoke Angelica's name, she would strike him with a braided whip. This would continue until he could either remember their name or admit he did not know, for not knowing she would place a special clamp around his genitals dangling chain and weighted ball. She would leave him there hanging from his wrists. She would return after a while and say to him this is how you feel when you think about Angelica, a room full of darkness, empty with only the salvation of pain, and she would lash him on the keywords Angelica and Pain before setting him free.

The letter ended here. Once again, it was constructed in a way to trigger Geremy's psyche along with the medication to deeply root it into his brain cells.

The last words in this letter like the first directed him to read every evening, with an added tidbit. Dr. Isnov is a liar.

Dr. Isnov was Geremy's one on one session psychiatrist.

Geremy once again did as directed; Meds at 8am... Breakfast at 9am... Group Therapy at 10am... Lunch at Noon... Fresh air outside at 1pm... Psych session at 2:30pm... Game room at 3:30pm... Meds at 5pm... Dinner at 6pm... Lockdown at 8pm. After lockdown, he would read the letters. Repeat... Repeat... Repeat.

During his one on one sessions when asked about Angelica, he would now get angry and talk about how she ruined his childhood and how her entire family made him feel subservient to them. This overly shy young man, whom at the peak of his adolescence and sexual curiosity had the most deeply felt crush on their daughter, became the families moldable putty figure.

Geremy's intermittent sparks of anger pleased Dr. Isnov, finally after half a year he was now starting to get somewhere, before this moment Geremy did not show any emotion nor would he admit to the raping and killing of Angelica. It was always the earthquake that took her life, and she wanted me to love her. This new Geremy is a layer folded back, and his anger is clear evidence of emotion towards why he is here. Dr. Isnov expressed to Geremy, "I think we are getting somewhere; you are starting to open up to discuss more of your feelings. I want to increase our one to one time, would you like that?". Geremy was non-responsive.

"Looking at your activity reports you seem to enjoy the outside time more than the Game room activities. If I removed the Game room time to increase outside time and our sessions, would you like that?" Geremy agreed by nodding his head.

Dr. Isnov placed the order for the new scheduling routine to begin the following week. There was still an area of Geremy's psychosis that Dr. Isnov failed to address or perhaps chose not too, that was the child. Geremy still has the firm belief that the child is his, and that the child will one day come to the same realization. For Dr. Isnov, the goal was to get Geremy to accept what he was committed for, to know it was wrong and to ship him off to the general population of the prison.

So, the following week, Geremy's schedule became:

Meds at 8am… Breakfast at 9am… Group Therapy at 10am… Lunch at Noon… Fresh air outside at 1pm… Psych session at 3:30pm… Meds at 5pm… Dinner at 6pm… Lockdown at 8pm. After lockdown, he would read the letters. Repeat… Repeat… Repeat.

Geremy grew stronger with more time in the yard, the sense of being captive grew less, and he thought more of finding Peter. His visits with Dr. Isnov became more conversational and Geremy started to lead most of the talks, still not giving enough to be sent to the general prison population. Geremy opened up to Dr. Isnov about the dark psychotic mind of Austin, and they discussed the dark side of sexual encounters. It was evident to Geremy that the good doctor was very interested and was a voyeur. Geremy met many voyeurs in his dark encounters, those that wanted too only watch and listen, too afraid to dive in fully but would play out small scenes when they could. Geremy would watch the doctors breathing patterns and the angle that he would sit in the chair as he unfolded the dark details of this world to him, often having to inform the doctor that their time together was over. Geremy began to notice the hold he was starting to have over the doctor. He thanked him for the extended outdoor time stating that it has helped him to open up more. He asked if the group therapy was still a necessary step in his development, he remarked that the increased outdoor and one to one time has proven to be more productive. Dr. Isnov agreed that Geremy was communicating better, feeding the doctors own personal fantasies, he shifted the daily schedule again.

Geremy's schedule now became:

Meds at 8am… Breakfast at 9am… Fresh air outside at 10am… Lunch at 11:30… Fresh air outside at 12:30pm… Psych session at 3pm… Meds at 5pm… Dinner at 6pm… Lockdown at 8pm. After lockdown, he would read the letters. Repeat… Repeat… Repeat.

This continued another week when a third unopened letter arrived, like the last two, the sender was again unknown to Geremy, but unlike the other letters, this letter did not have a bashing from Austin in the beginning. In fact, this letter started with a compliment.

I see that you have gotten stronger and have learned how to use the teachings of becoming a Master over your Slave on Dr. Isnov, Very Good, but remember to stay dominant the slave needs to have something with them as a constant reminder of your presence. You will find blank pages in this letter, write an experience down for the doctor and tell him it was a dream you had, include him in the fantasy, give him an active role. Tell him you wrote it down so that you would not forget it and when you present it to him gently grab his hand and tell him it seemed so real, what do you think the dream was trying to tell me? If he ends your session, you've got him, he will run off to read the letter. If he continues your one to one, you must get more forceful and aggressive, tell him to return the letter to you and rip it twice and throw it at him. On your next session, apologize for your behavior and tell him that you are sorry for ripping up the letter and that you wish he could have read it so that you could have discussed it together. Most likely, he will show you the taped together letter, then you will look him in his eyes and say to him, "you did read it, please keep it with you always." Allow him to finish the session with you thinking he has control over you.

And continue your upcoming sessions in the same manner that you were doing before this letter.

This letter ended with no instruction informing him to read every evening.

Dr. Isnov after receiving the letter, continued the session. Geremy performed a fit of anger telling the doctor, "I took the time to write this for you, and you just discard it, give it back to me." Geremy stood and removed the letter from the desk, ripped it twice, and threw it at the doctor. The guards rushed in and constrained Geremy, Dr. Isnov ordered him back to his room on lockdown. After everyone had left the room, he picked up the torn pieces of the letter, and instead of placing it into the patient folder, he put it into his pocket.

Geremy remained in lockdown throughout the night and the next day until it was time for his one to one session. He was brought to the next session handcuffed, Dr. Isnov had the guards remove the restraints and sit Geremy in the chair, before the doctor could say anything Geremy apologized for his previous behavior. He told the doctor that he felt rejected by him not reading the letter when he gave it to him. Dr. Isnov then apologized to Geremy for reflecting the appearance of dismissal as he removed the letter from his pocket, Geremy could see that he had taped the letter back together. He told Geremy, "I found that your placement of me in an active role while you stayed in the background and watched, an area that we should explore deeper. In the roles that you have shared with me so far, you have always been an active participant, have you ever just watched."

"No, I haven't, which is why I wrote it down to bring to you, this dream was completely out of character for me."

"Can you remember the emotion that it left you with or that you were experiencing during the dream?"

"No, it was a dream, and now, I am awake."

"Would you allow me to place you under hypnosis, it could relax you enough to have the dream again."

"Oh no, you're not putting me under."

"It's ok, let's talk some more and maybe it will come to you. You said after having the dream you wrote it down because the role in the dream was out of character. What was your hope, that by showing it to me, that I would do with it?"

"Help me to understand it. It reminded me of a feeling that I drove out of my head years ago, a feeling of being subservient."

"In your dream, with me having the active role, was your subservience to me!"

"That's what was puzzling to me. In the dream you were my Slave, but I felt and saw the dream as though I was you – the slave."

"Have you ever held the role of a Master or wanted to be a one."

"No"

"Well perhaps then because in reality not having played the role of a Master nor a desire to become one, your dream state could not create one. The only reference in your psyche was that of a slave.

On that admission, Dr. Isnov ended the session and placed the letter back in his pocket.

As a voyeur, Dr. Isnov never knew the real impact of being a Slave or a Master. Now before him, he had a Slave-making his transition to becoming a Master. He imagined that this could be his transitioning point as well, to becoming a Slave, a Slave to Geremy. How could that ever work Geremy is in here for 18 more months, and then he will be moved into the general population whether he understands the reason for his sentencing or not. Then he thought maybe I won't like being in the role of a Slave, having Geremy placed in the general prison system would be my way back out. This is starting to be a great scenario if I want out at any time all I have to do is sign a paper, and Geremy would be gone. But, What if he turns me and I lose my will to go against him – what then? The doctor thought back on most of the Slaves that he had witnessed, after the roleplay, they would go about their everyday jobs with no impact on their performance. For Geremy and I, if the fetish started to jeopardize my performance and I would need to end it, then this would be a battle of my mind over my desires. Right now, my voyeurism is my desire and amongst the many times that I have tried to stop, I still cannot. Would replacing voyeurism with becoming a Slave be the same. If I became a Slave, and Geremy transfers to the prison system, I would become a Slave without a Master. What then, back to a voyeur, would I just transfer to someone else or would I be left with a void that can never again be fulfilled, an emptiness that no one can help me with. Similar to a woman suffering a traumatic loss of her child during birthing returning to the hospital emergency room night after night claiming that she is it's time for her baby to be delivered. Or a man caught in an explosion rendering him unconscious losing his limbs and blinded by the event, waking up in the darkness forever bedridden with the feeling that his arms and legs are still there thinking he's just not strong enough to lift them. These are exasperating mental conditions of mind over desire and reality. This is why I have never gone any further than watching, am I mentally strong enough to separate the fetish playing from the real world. Why am I feeling this strong urge to pursue it now and why with this guy?

The next day Dr. Isnov canceled his session with Geremy and allowed him to spend that time in the yard. When Geremy returned to his cell, he was given another letter from an unknown sender. The letter read Geremy you have done an exceptional job on Dr. Isnov, I am proud of your progress now it is time to remove you from your current surroundings. Dr. Isnov will be out again tomorrow and while you are in your afternoon yard session, I want you to walk out of the yard door and straight to the fence only look forward, Once at the fence I want you to count to 25 and slowly move to the far-right corner of the yard, stand close to the fence but DO NOT TOUCH it. LOOK DOWN.

The letter ended.

Geremy placed this letter with the others, a little perplexed as to its reference for removing him from his current surroundings. He thought that perhaps he may have pushed the doctor to hard, and he signed the paperwork to have him shipped to the prison population thus revealing the ultimate goal of the unknown sender. Why were Austin's words not present in the last two letters? Geremy was starting to lose trust in this unknown mentor. How does this person know such detail on the fetishes - the small peculiarities that even he had blocked out. His mind grew weary of all these thoughts, it was time to sleep and see what tomorrow will bring.

Geremy started his day in the same manner as every other day; Meds at 8am... Breakfast at 9am... Fresh air outside at 10am... Lunch at 11:30... then as the letter predicted he was informed that he would have another extended period in the yard. Geremy did as directed he walk forward straight to the fence and gazed outward counting slowly to 25 then he slowly walked to the far-right corner and looked down. There written in chalk like children playing in the street were the words:

fence is cut

push it forward

run around the corner

NOW!

Geremy pushed on the fence and started running. There were three other inmates in the yard, and after seeing Geremy, they ran to the opening and through the fence. Their running alerted the guards, and the alarms of escape rang through the air, several armed guards ran out of the same opening in pursuit. When Geremy turned the corner, there was a car parked at the next intersection with the door open. He ran and got in, while still in the motion of shutting the door, they drove off. Geremy did not recognize the driver, and as he looked to his left to see his travel companion, he was surprised to find out it was his Dommes sitting there in her leather holding his mask. He took the mask and put it on, then rested his head on her lap. She told him that he was a good learner, and now he must complete his teachings and feel the ultimate joy of undeniable sex. She said to him that Austin would not be able to help him on this part of his journey.

The truth about Austin is that he met an untimely demise; he was killed in his prison cell by a relative of the girl murdered on the kayaking trip, his balls were cut out and shoved down his throat, and he was left there to bleed to death.

The Dommes in the real world is the Director of Prison Psychiatrics Nationwide. Psychiatry is a flawed field, after hearing the mental cries of others, you have to find a place to offload it. You don't bring it home to give to a loved one cause then it will be rehashed over and over again as they search for a rational way to accept it or a mental place to store it, you don't share it with friends. No, for a psychiatrist the only solution is another psychiatrist, the psychiatrist's psychiatrist. The Dommes setup a small network of such professionals within the prison system, and she became the psychiatrist's psychiatrist to them, this was her way of monitoring and controlling the system and treatments.

Geremy was taken to one of the Dommes' secret Dominatrix houses seclude in the rural areas of Northern California. By the time of his escape Geremy, had become very skillful at the arts of a Master, a fact that was not known by the Dommes because Dr. Isnov left this out of his reports and his sessions with the psychiatrist's psychiatrist. He was afraid of losing his job if anyone found out about his fetish desires. The Dommes knew about his situation because she had encountered him several times in the fetish rooms.

Geremy knew how to play the slave role to the Dommes, seeing as she was his emancipator. Her initial hold on Geremy was Angelica, but with her death, Geremy has a much stronger element driving him beyond the Dommes control. This one element for Geremy is like Popeye's spinach, Samson's hair, and Thor's hammer it's the strength to resist the Dommes or to possess her. The one element he has never lost sight of, his child – Peter.

It's time to find Peter, but this time he knew he could not use the traditional means, I'm a wanted fugitive, this time I will take him when the time is right. For now, I will let the Dommes have her way with me and keep me safe, as we search out a suitable suitor to complete the ultimate sexual pleasure on my way to becoming the new Austin.

Meanwhile at Harry's house…

Knock Knock Knock!!; Knock Knock Knock!! Coming, I'm coming.

Harry opens the door – "Carl, what are you doing here and what's with all of the law enforcement. "

"Harry, please let us in."

Harry moves away from the door, Carl and Dave sit down. Margarite enters from the bedroom.

"Carl, what are you doing here."

"Hi Sis, you better sit down also."

"What is it?"

"It's Geremy. He's escaped, and we fear he may be coming for Peter."